"Kiss me," he begged, and Preston's mouth on his, invading, taking ownership, was a heaven he would never have guessed.

WELCOME TO

DREAMSPUN DESIRES

Dear Reader,

Love is the dream. It dazzles us, makes us stronger, and brings us to our knees. Dreamspun Desires tell stories of love featuring your favorite heartwarming heroes, captivating plots, and exotic locations. Stories that make your breath catch and your imagination soar.

In the pages of these wonderful love stories, readers can escape to a world where love conquers all, the tenderness of a first kiss sweeps you away, and your heart pounds at the sight of the one you love.

When you put it all together, you find romance in its truest form.

Love always finds a way.

Elizabeth North

Executive Director
Dreamspinner Press

Amy Lane

SILENT HEART

PUBLISHED BY

REAMSPINNER
PRESS

Published by
DREAMSPINNER PRESS

5032 Capital Circle SW, Suite 2, PMB# 279,
Tallahassee, FL 32305-7886 USA
www.dreamspinnerpress.com

This is a work of fiction. Names, characters, places, and incidents either
are the product of author imagination or are used fictitiously, and any
resemblance to actual persons, living or dead, business establishments,
events, or locales is entirely coincidental.

Silent Heart
© 2020 Amy Lane
Editorial Development by Sue Brown-Moore

Cover Art
© 2020 Alexandria Corza
http://www.seeingstatic.com/
Cover content is for illustrative purposes only and any person depicted
on the cover is a model.

Paperback ISBN: 978-1-64108-239-6
Digital ISBN: 978-1-64405-813-8
Library of Congress Control Number: 2019949980
Paperback published January 2020
v. 1.0

Printed in the United States of America
∞
This paper meets the requirements of
ANSI/NISO Z39.48-1992 (Permanence of Paper).

AMY LANE lives in a crumbling crapmansion with two teenagers, a passel of furbabies, and a bemused spouse. She's been a finalist in the RITAs™ twice, has won honorable mention for an Indiefab, and has a couple of Rainbow Awards to her name. She also has too damned much yarn, a penchant for action-adventure movies, and a need to know that somewhere in all the pain is a story of Wuv, Twu Wuv, which she continues to believe in to this day! She writes fantasy, urban fantasy, mystery/suspense, and contemporary romance—and if you accidentally make eye contact, she'll bore you to tears with literary theory. She'll also tell you that sacrifices, large and small, are worth the urge to write.

Website: www.greenshill.com
Blog: www.writerslane.blogspot.com
Email: amylane@greenshill.com
Facebook: www.facebook.com/amy.lane.167
Twitter: @amymaclane

By Amy Lane

DREAMSPUN DESIRES
THE MANNIES
The Virgin Manny
Manny Get Your Guy
Stand by Your Manny
A Fool and His Manny

SEARCH AND RESCUE
Warm Heart
Silent Heart

Published by **DREAMSPINNER PRESS**
www.dreamspinnerpress.com

Mate, Mary, Rayna, kids—
and Elizabeth. Because ((hugs)).

Acknowledgments

THANKS to the folks who talked to me about Preston, and to Sue who helped me Newt Scamander a character who doesn't get written as much as he should. And to Chicken, because plotting with her is the best.

Silent Heart

DAMIEN Ward scowled as he pulled his battered truck up next to the private hangar outside of Napa Valley. The hangar was small, housing one Cessna 182, one Cessna Grand Caravan, one deluxe refurbished Black Hawk passenger helicopter specially outfitted with soundproofing and medical equipment, and one AS350 B3e helicopter that was currently out on a mission.

All four aircraft were painted an elegant eggshell color with a green lizard on the side, part of the logo that read Gecko Inc., the private rescue service run by Damien and his partner, Glen Echo, call sign Gecko.

Glen was the one out in the AS350.

Still out on a goddamned mission.

He should have been back yesterday.

As Damien turned the truck off, leaped out, and hurried for the small door in the side of the hangar, an equally battered Ford F-150 pulled to a stop next to his truck, and Damien repressed a groan.

Shit. He'd hoped to have some news before Preston got here, but he'd underestimated Preston's ability to drive like a bat out of hell.

He had not, however, underestimated the ability of Glen's little brother to disturb his libido. It wasn't easy as he watched the rangy young man emerge from his vehicle, feet planted one at a time, and whistle sharply for Preacher, a hundred short-haired, block-headed pounds of his favorite dog. Damien tried to ignore the little punch of longing that hit him right in the solar plexus. Preston had wheat-gold hair and sky-blue eyes and a rectangular square-jawed face right out of a superhero movie—but it was more than the fact that he looked like every Chris and Steve on the screen.

Preston moved with an unconscious grace and an absolute focus. Every movement was about getting him from point A to point B with as little extra motion as possible. His brain was like that too. The most direct route to the most useful conclusion.

It was something Damien really admired about him—and feared a little too.

Damien's own conclusions about himself these days were pretty straightforward and pretty painful. Hearing the obvious come out of Preston's mouth would destroy him.

"He's not here yet," Preston said, lowering his hand to Preacher's head and rubbing his ears rhythmically.

"I know," Damien said as he pulled out his keys and opened the door.

"He was supposed to be back last night."

"I know." The office was dark, just as it had been after Glen took off three days before. The desk sat in the corner, paperwork neatly in the outbox, laptop turned off and unplugged to save energy. Any business calls would be routed to Glen's and Damien's cell phones, since they were mostly out of the office anyway. While Gecko Inc., their independent search-and-rescue firm, was their baby, depending on people who needed to be rescued and had families willing to pay for beyond-the-usual government services was not really a good source of steady income. The three-seater was used in aerial tours of the Bay Area, and the Black Hawk and Cessnas were frequently used to shuttle people from point A to point B with a minimum of fuss.

Damien himself was most often employed by a startup firm that helped get athletes off the ground and into the pro circuit of their specialty. Damien had been shuttling Mallory Armstrong and his husband, Tevyn, to Tevyn's house in Colorado when Glen had gotten the call.

It hadn't been an emergency, really. In Glen's words, "Some punk kid got himself in a jam and fell off the grid in Mexico. I know where he was last, and I've got a friend who's got a probable location. I'll go check it out."

Damien had told him to wait—they could both go down. He'd only been three hours away, but Glen, stubborn bastard, had been convinced he could be in and out in forty-eight hours.

Twelve hours in, he'd called and said he had the kid, they were negotiating a truce, and Glen would have him back in a day. Damien hadn't wanted to ask about the "negotiating a truce" part. For one thing, he wasn't sure what the war between Glen and this particular "punk kid" was about, and for another? Glen was not necessarily a diplomat.

Damien hadn't wanted to point out that the reason they'd both been honorably discharged from the service was that Glen had threatened a CO with bodily harm if he didn't let Glen and Damien go back and retrieve a fallen soldier. The CO had refused, Glen and Damien had done it anyway, and it had taken Damien's quiet threat to have the man brought up on charges of cowardice to keep them both from a court-martial.

So Damien had been worried and had offered to take the Black Hawk to Puerto Vallarta so Glen would have backup, but Glen had flat-out refused.

"I'll be damned if I let this little bastard call the shots," he'd muttered, and Damien had just stepped back. There was no talking to Gecko when he got this cold-blooded. Fifteen years of friendship told Damien that.

But twelve hours after that contact, Damien had called again, and Glen's blistering tirade about entitled little assholes who thought they knew everything had been cut off by a dropped signal.

There'd been an earthquake in the area, and Glen hadn't responded to Damien's frantic calls over the last few hours. Damien had filed the flight plan from his phone and called Preston en route to the hangar.

But Damien and Glen lived in Burlingame, and Preston lived on a stretch of undeveloped farmland about twenty miles in the other direction from the hangar. Damien hadn't counted on traffic—or the fact that Preston probably had a go-bag packed at all times and had probably repacked it when his brother had failed to call.

Damien plugged in the laptop and flipped it open, then lowered himself carefully into the desk chair, keeping his face blank. His leg was 85 percent functional now—but that 15 percent missing came with a lot of pain and stiffness, and he didn't like to complain.

"What are you doing?" Preston asked loudly, and Damien startled a little, because the office was a quiet cubicle in the vast echo chamber of the hangar.

"Looking up your brother's flight plan," Damien said. "And the supply manifest in the Black Hawk and the Cessna."

"Which one are we taking?"

Damien had filed the plan for the Caravan because he knew some of the smaller airstrips in the area, and Preston and his dog were more comfortable in the larger plane. He had a feeling the Black Hawk's ability to land in a tighter place might be useful—too bad the damned thing was like a tank being lifted by a hummingbird, though, so he would have to worry about fuel a lot sooner.

"The Caravan," Damien said briefly. "You can start loading your stuff and let Preacher get a good sniff around it. It's been fueled up, but I think we may need to load some of the supplies from the Black Hawk into the luggage compartment. I want to be ready for everything."

Preston grunted. "Are you?" he asked baldly.

"Am I what?"

"Ready for everything?"

Damien swallowed. "It's impossible to be ready for everything, Preston. You know that. I just want to try—"

"I don't mean supplies," Preston said. "I mean you."

"The leg can take it," he said evenly. A trip that long would be rough, but he'd been good at setting the autopilot and stretching once an hour to keep himself from cramping up.

"I didn't know the leg was a problem, which pisses me off," Preston muttered. "But that's not my question. Are you still afraid to fly?"

Shit. "I'm not afraid to fly," he lied. "I flew back from Colorado yesterday, remember? I make my life in the air—"

Preston growled, like one of the dogs he spent so much of his time with. "Don't lie to me," he said. "My brother is missing, and he can't rescue us if something goes wrong!"

"I don't need rescuing!" Damien burst out. "I'm fine. I can get us there, and we'll find him, and everything will be fine."

"Everything is not fine!" Preston shouted. "Glen is gone, and you haven't been the same since the crash. If everything was fine, we'd be having sex when we're together, but it's not, so we're not, and I'm tired of it. I don't want sex *right* now, but I really want to find my brother!"

Damien scrubbed at his face with his hand. Emotional evasion—he was great at it. Preston, on the other hand, was the opposite. "Uh, Preston, that's a lot to unpack—"

"It's all true," Preston said stubbornly.

"You're my partner's brother," Damien said patiently. "A relationship would be problematic. I told you that last year—"

"Glen said you were lying," Preston said, surprising him. "He said you were lying because you didn't want to talk about what was really wrong. He said I had to wait for you. I've waited. I'm bored waiting. And now we have to find Glen, and I need to know if you're all right." His fair skin was flushed and blotchy on his cheeks and neck, and he had the same irritated look Glen got whenever Damien said he was fine. Or lately, whenever Glen made some sort of snarky comment and Damien had no comeback. Last week, Damien's best friend had told him he was as much fun as a battery acid enema.

Great. Brothers. Go figure.

"My leg is stiff," Damien said, deciding the truth would get them out of the hangar sooner. "But it will be fine. And as for that other thing, I can fly just fine. Recertified before I got back in the saddle, remember?" He'd thrown up for an hour after he'd landed. He hadn't told anybody that, not even Glen. "I'm not going to hide in the corner right now when your brother needs me—you get that, don't you?"

"Sure," Preston snapped. "You hide in the corner when *I* need you but not when my brother needs you."

"You've never needed me," Damien said sadly. "I know that, Preston. You're okay without me."

Preston looked past Damien's ear, his face set without expression. "I lied that day," he said. "I didn't know it was lying, but I lied." He shook himself and put his hand down on top of Preacher's head again.

"We've got to get moving," Damien told him, hoping to end this moment, this painful, confusing moment, before either one of them said something they couldn't take back.

"I'll go load stuff," Preston said. "But we'll be in the plane for hours, Damien. You'll have to talk to me sometime."

"Sure." Damien rubbed his stomach. "I'm going to hit the head and start looking through supplies."

Preston gave him five minutes before he barged into the bathroom, using the master key he'd gotten from the office. He found Damien on his knees during what had become his preflight ritual, tossing his cookies into the commode.

Preston stood at the doorway and watched expressionlessly as Damien finished, for which Damien was grateful. Some people might have offered a hand on the head or the back, which would have been sweet, but frankly Damien didn't want to be touched.

Damien went to the sink and washed up, then finished up with toothpaste and turned back toward the door. Preston was still regarding him with lowered brows.

"What's wrong?" Preston asked.

"Got sick." Damien hoped that would do it, but as he watched Preston's hand come down for Preacher's head again, he realized that of all people, Preston would get the physical response to the strong emotion.

"Why?" Preston asked, expression not moving.

"I just do. Come on. I want to finish up so we can go. Reports coming out of Jalisco and Nayarit are saying that some of the smaller outlying villages in the area have been really damaged by the quake. We may need to contact emergency workers and let them know to look out for your brother and Cash Harper—"

"The punk kid?" Preston clarified.

"Yeah. He's the guy your brother was supposed to go get. Anyway, we've got to…."

He approached the doorway, but Preston didn't move.

Damien's breath caught. Preston spent entire weeks out training with his dogs, running around the property in Napa that he and Glen had inherited from their grandparents. His body was rangy, muscular, and always seemed to smell just a little bit of the out of doors and pleasant exertion.

And his chest was as wide as a truck and right now looked as unbreakable as a brick wall.

"Preston?" he said uncertainly.

"Talk to me," Preston said, his voice thready with hurt. "My whole life, you've been the one person who would talk to me. You were never afraid of me, never afraid of the things I might say. You used to talk too fucking much, but that was fine. Comforting. Ever since the accident, you don't talk at all—and especially not to me. Other people, maybe, but not Glen and me. Why are you getting sick? Why isn't your leg getting better? Why won't you *talk to me*?"

Damien looked into his face with a mixture of fear and yearning. A year and a half ago, before the helicopter crash that had nearly taken Damien's leg, he'd longed for Preston to look him in the eyes and tell him in some way, any way, that Damien was special.

But after the crash, Preston had grown remote and alien, like he was afraid to talk to Damien the way they had before, and Damien?

Damien had been a mess. Who wanted to get into a relationship with a guy learning to walk again? A pilot afraid to fly?

Damien had thrown himself into recovery and bid thoughts of Preston, of the half-articulated hopes he'd had, goodbye.

But Preston was standing in front of him, keeping him from going to Glen, and Damien had a hard enough time staying as cold and distant to Preston as Preston had been to him.

"Why does it matter?" he asked bitterly. "We need to get your brother, and I'm the pilot to do it. Why does it matter if my leg will *never* be the same, or flying makes me break into a cold sweat before I go up?"

"You used to love to fly," Preston said, stoic mask relaxing, eyes expressive. "You told me it was your one wonderful thing."

Damien shook his head, that moment in the air etched behind his eyes and needing no excuses to intrude and make him panic. "So were you," he said, feeling miserable. "But you didn't want me. Now can we go? Your brother needs us."

He didn't want to touch Preston without his permission. Preston *liked* hands on his shoulders, hard tight hugs. Preston was unashamed of infringing on personal space, but consent and permission had been drilled into him from an early age. Nobody touched him without his consent, and he gave the world the same consideration.

So what Preston said next shocked him. "I'm going to hug you now. Don't startle."

Damien's eyes flew open, and Preston wrapped strong arms around his shoulders.

Don't Startle

DAMIEN had taught Preston about how friends hugged.

Preston's brother, Glen, was eight years older than him, which meant Preston had been eleven when Glen had gone off to the Air Force, and thirteen when he'd come home with his friend Damien in tow.

The men had stayed on Preston's grandmother's property for a month that summer. They'd helped clear fields and build fire breaks, as well as built fences and reroofed the house itself. Preston had tagged along with them, and Glen had trusted him with a hammer and nails, and even driving the truck, as long as it was on the property, and Preston had felt wanted and useful and interesting.

Glen's friend Damien had been the most beautiful man Preston had ever seen.

Black hair, tawny skin, kind almond-shaped brown eyes. Even his lips had been perfect—not too full, not too lean. Everything Damien was, Preston wanted.

Preston hadn't had words for it then—barely had them now—but Damien had held the attraction of a lodestone. Wherever on the property Damien had been, Preston had pointed.

Once, when they thought Preston was back at the house, he'd heard Glen asking if Damien was tired of having a shadow yet. Damien had replied that no, he found Preston's company soothing.

"He doesn't yammer, and he listens," Damien had said.

"You talk more than any person I know!" Glen laughed.

"Yes, but I don't *say* anything." Damien had laughed too, and Preston had spent the rest of the afternoon wondering how a person could talk a lot but not say anything. He figured that if anybody could do that, it was Damien and his brother—they bantered, insulted, bitched, and chattered enough to make Preston put his hands over his ears, and much of it had two meanings, which Preston had trouble understanding.

But he hadn't felt rejected, and he hadn't felt awkward, and Damien's halo grew, if anything, a little shinier.

Glen continued to bring Damien with him whenever they had leave together. One summer evening when Preston was fifteen, he overheard Glen and his mother talking while he was sitting on the porch, checking his grandmother's massive Labrador mixes for ticks.

"Son, you and Damien aren't… you know, a thing, are you?"

"If you're asking if we're gay? Yes. If you're asking if we're dating? No. We never… you know. Clicked that way."

Preston heard the pause and wondered what his mother was thinking.

"So you're gay?" she asked, her voice squeaking.

"Yeah. Do you want us to leave?" Glen was what his mother called "blunt." Preston was also blunt, but he usually managed to horrify his mother and grandmother with *his* bluntness.

"No! No, honey. Just, you know, had to let it sink in. I wouldn't have asked if I hadn't been ready for the answer."

"So Damien can stay too?"

"Well, yes—we love having him come here. Does he not like going home?"

Glen grunted. "His parents aren't great with him being gay," he said. "And they're even worse with him being in the military. He likes it here."

"Well, good. And frankly, it's good that Preston has the two of you."

"Why?"

"Hey, Preston!" Damien said, striding from the direction of the barn, which was around the house. "How you doing, kid?"

Preston startled, arms going out, head coming up, like a baby moved too fast. Cletus, his grandmother's most easygoing dog, gave a startled *whuff* and trotted off.

"Whoa! Preston! What's wrong?"

Preston sighed. "My mother was talking about me," he said, working hard on voice modulation. It was something he practiced during his special day class at school. How to have the appropriate voice for the appropriate surroundings.

"Oh." Damien dropped his voice automatically. "Sorry. What was she saying?"

Preston looked over his shoulder and saw that the window had cleared and his mother and Glen had moved to another part of the house.

"She was telling him why I got in trouble today," Preston said glumly.

Damien whistled. "I forget you guys are in school this late. Bummer. Why did you get in trouble today? Your teachers usually love you!"

"I was inappropriate to Ozzy." He cleaned the dog brush disconsolately, rolling the dog fur into a ball.

"Isn't Ozzy your best friend?"

Yes. Ozzy was in the special class because he had dyslexia. Preston learned how to modulate his voice, and Ozzy got extra time to listen to books on tape. But Ozzy said the books were boring and he'd rather talk to Preston.

"Yes," Preston confirmed. "We were sitting next to each other, listening to one of his books. He smelled *really* good. I told him that, and he laughed. So I tried to kiss him."

Damien made a strange sound, and Preston looked at his pretty face quickly, checking his expression, running it through the practice expressions he used during SDC. "What is that face?" he asked suspiciously.

"You surprised me," Damien told him. "I didn't know you were gay."

"Neither did Ozzy," Preston said shortly. He rolled Cletus's fur into a tighter ball. "And he hit me because he was surprised."

"Aw, Preston. I'm sorry. Did he get in trouble?"

Preston shook his head, still looking at that perfectly round ball of dog hair. "No. Because before the teacher could get mad, Ozzy said, 'I'm sorry! I'm sorry! You startled me! I'm sorry, Preston. I'm not gay, but can we still be friends?'"

"Oh wow," Damien said, sitting next to him on the white-painted porch. Preston kept rolling the dog hair, but now he was looking at Damien's thighs.

They were very nicely shaped, he thought. Compact and highly defined. He was wearing cargo shorts and a thin T-shirt. Preston stared at the middle of that T-shirt and wondered what his skin felt like under it.

His own skin started to tingle around his nipples and his groin, and he sighed. He'd had erections before, and he knew why they occurred, but he didn't want to have that discussion with Damien.

"Oh wow what?" Preston asked.

"Oh wow, that's important. What did you say?" Damien asked, his voice soft and sort of fuzzy.

"I said yes," Preston told him, surprised. "Why would I take it personal if Ozzy didn't want to kiss me? He still wanted to be my friend."

"Yes, he did," Damien said. "And that's important. You want to treat a friend like that really good."

Preston looked up and risked eye contact. Damien's eyes were kind, and his lips were pulled up in the corners, like he was happy with Preston.

Oh, that was such a relief. His teacher had not been happy *at all*.

"That's what I told him," Preston said. "And the teacher told me that you couldn't kiss people without permission, and Ozzy said he wasn't mad. But they had to send a note home explaining why I had a bruise on my cheek, and Mom was… difficult to understand," he said. Until he'd overheard her talking to Glen, he hadn't been sure if he'd been in trouble for liking Ozzy or not.

"Well, parents are often difficult to understand," Damien told him. "I don't get mine at all."

"Glen said they don't like that you're gay, but they really don't like that you're in the military."

Damien's mouth twisted. "Something like that. Has anybody told you that listening under windows is bad?"

"All the time," Preston replied. "I do it anyway. It's a dumb rule."

Damien laughed, and Preston's stomach warmed. Oh, he liked that sound!

"It's a polite rule," he corrected. "But given who your brother is, I don't expect you to know that."

"Glen isn't polite?" This was news to Preston—he thought Glen was perfect—but Damien's even deeper laugh told him that Damien had a different experience.

"Glen's the rudest jackass I've ever met," Damien said when he could breathe. "Oh my God, he can't open his mouth without pissing someone off. I once bet him a steak dinner he couldn't keep quiet for a puddle-jump between San Francisco and Sacramento. I ate steak that night, Preston, believe me!"

Preston's smile was always a little scary to him because smiling happened without his control. Times like this, it seemed to take over his face.

"He lost the bet!"

"Yes, he did!"

"What did he talk about?"

Damien snorted softly. "Something you're still a little young to know about."

"I know about sex," Preston said. "We've had sex-ed four years running."

"Well, good for you, but *I'm* too young to be telling you what he was talking about, and we'll leave it at that. Anyway, your brother talks too much, and he tells inappropriate jokes. So don't worry about living up to Glen, buddy. You just keep being you."

Oh, talking to Damien—always a joy—was *not* getting any worse. For a moment, Preston laughed, but then he remembered the thing that had really bothered him about the altercation with Ozzy.

"What's wrong?" Damien asked, that kindness in his voice still. "You got sad again."

"I really wanted to kiss someone," Preston said on a sigh. "How am I going to get to kiss someone if I'm not allowed to do it?"

"Well, for one thing, kissing in school is inappropriate."

"Other kids do it." That pissed Preston off.

"Yes, but you're better than that. You only kiss where it's appropriate—and if anybody tries to get you to make out during class, you use that line, okay?"

"Fine." But it was disappointing.

"Which brings us to the other thing. If you are hanging with another boy, and you'd like to kiss him, ask his permission. You're always so honest. Don't stop. Say, 'I'd like to kiss you, but I won't do anything without your consent.'"

And a big lightbulb went off in Preston's head. "We talk about consent all the time!" And now it made sense.

"Yes. Exactly."

"So if I wanted to kiss *you*—"

Damien held up his hands. "I am too old for you, Preston. And that would be inappropriate."

Preston sighed, his shoulders slumping. "That's depressing," he said.

"Here, kid," Damien said. "I'm going to put my arm around your shoulders. I still don't want to kiss you, but I want to be your friend. Is that okay?"

"Yes," Preston said, accepting that Damien had been honest with him and he shouldn't push that boundary—not now.

"Good." Damien's arm was so comforting, Preston forgave him for saying no to the kiss.

"Wanting to kiss someone is so confusing," he said, his disheartenment obvious.

"Yeah, kid. I know. Here, I'm going to hug you for a sec. Don't startle."

Damien put both arms around him, and Preston rested his cares and his confusion on Damien's strong shoulders.

And he breathed deeply, because that helped him to relax.

Damien smelled so good.

DAMIEN smelled good now too—but he smelled different. The sun smell and the hay smell were gone, and in their place was sweat and a faint cologne. He melted into Preston's chest, boneless and warm, as though he trusted Preston to carry the weight of his cares and confusion like Preston had trusted him twelve years ago.

Preston had gotten a *lot* of sex since then.

Damien's advice had proved incredibly sound. Just telling boys, "I would really like to kiss you, but I won't do anything without consent," had helped lessen the confusion. Yes, sometimes boys got hostile, but once the word got out that Preston was gay—and over six feet tall with a chest like a tank—those boys didn't hang out with him anymore. That hurt, yes, but it also made high school and college very clear-cut. His friends would be his friends, and the other people weren't let into his heart.

That was comforting.

This hug was the opposite of comforting. Preston's nipples began to tingle and his groin too, and he'd had enough sex, and enough hugs, to know that that original feeling he'd had for Damien—the one that had made him Preston's lodestone so no matter where Damien went that was the way Preston pointed—that hadn't gone away.

For a moment, Preston thought about pulling back, but he remembered Damien's pale face, the way he had always smiled before the accident, and how now he had no expression, like he was holding them all in his head, and he thought Damien had probably had a lot of sex too.

Damien wouldn't care if Preston had an erection, right?

But when Damien's thigh brushed up against Preston's groin, Damien gave a little shimmy. He leaned back enough to look at Preston's face.

"Really?" he asked, surprised enough to let some of the old Damien through.

"I have never stopped wanting to kiss you," Preston said, refusing to be uncomfortable.

"But after the accident—"

Damien's pocket let out a chirp, followed by a "Danger Zone" ringtone. Damien pulled back and jerked his phone out, his hands obviously shaking, and then he swore.

"Glen?" Preston asked anxiously.

"The call dropped." Damien pressed a few buttons and then speaker, but there was no message on the voicemail, and he swore.

Another chirp, and he frowned at the screen.

"What's it say?" Preston asked.

"*Bring supplies goddammit. Fucking Nayarit.*"

A rather stunned silence hung between them before Damien smirked.

"My brother is an asshat," Preston said, because that about covered it. "What's wrong with Nayarit?"

"Not a damned thing," Damien muttered. "I *like* Jalisco and Nayarit. But the supplies…." He grimaced. "The earthquake. He must want to help. Damn, I should have thought of that."

"You were worried," Preston told him. "The last time one of you disappeared, you almost died."

Damien gave him a look.

Preston wasn't sure what *sort* of look, but it was very much *a look*.

"I could have gone the entire day without you mentioning that," Damien said sincerely.

"I don't know why. We're both thinking about it every goddamned minute."

Damien's mouth dropped, like he'd said something shocking, but Preston thought it was only the truth. "Did he text anything else?"

Damien let out a grunt of frustration. "Yeah. *Battery dead.*"

And for once they were on the same page. "What. An. Asshole," Preston said at the same time Damien said, "*Ass. Hole.*"

They both took a deep breath, the kind that helped them steady their temper. "So Nayarit isn't bad?" Preston asked.

"Nice beaches, condos, nice people, good food," Damien confirmed. "Buddy lives there—you remember him from that case with the hiker?"

Preston remembered. Most places had their own rescue dogs, but Preston got called out about six times a year, usually to places where the authorities regarded the certainty of a trained dog with the deep suspicion of witchcraft. They'd known Buddy for a while, and Buddy had called them out on the job a couple of times—Preston in particular—because there simply hadn't been an association of trained dogs nearby. "Yes," he said. "Buddy and Martha—they were kind."

Damien smiled briefly. "Yeah, they were. He's Glen's contact, tracking down this Cash Harper kid." He looked troubled. "I hope they haven't been hit too hard by the quake. Here—tell you what. I'll put the plane through flight check, and you take Preacher downtown and get supplies. I'll send you a list. The survival place is closed today, but Walmart should have what we need."

Preston nodded. If they knew Glen was okay—at least for now—he could take a minute to breathe.

"We'll still have the whole flight to talk," he warned Damien.

"Believe me," Damien muttered, "I know."

PRESTON had an orange vest for Preacher in the truck—one of many. Preacher was one of the dogs he took to the special school as a therapy dog twice a month, so Preacher's was a little bit worn and a little more wrinkled by grubby hands.

Preacher wasn't *really* being of service today—but Preston didn't want to leave him in the back of the truck, and Preacher was too well-trained to act up in public.

Preston traveled up and down the concrete walkways of Walmart, his face set, his mission firmly implanted. Water, granola bars, packets of nuts, plain oatmeal, jerky, gauze, disinfectant, wet wipes, toilet paper, and beach towels. If the survivalist store had been open, Preston would have gotten fire retardant Mylar blankets, which packed really small and conveniently. They were closed on Sunday, though, so Preston grabbed the thin, brightly colored beach towels by the handful and hoped there were no fires. By the time he was done, he had three carts ready to take through checkout, and if it wasn't for Preacher's hopeful little twitch of the eyebrows, he might have forgotten the most important thing.

"Treats?" he asked Preacher gently. In response, Preacher allowed his bright pink tongue to loll in his chocolate-brindled face.

Preston smiled at his best friend and scratched him behind the ears, then grabbed the bag of soft-meat treats that Preacher loved best of all. With any luck, Preacher would get the whole bag to himself for just sitting and calming people down, but Preston had been training dogs since he was a little kid. His grandmother had helped lead search-and-rescue teams with dogs when he, Glen, and his mother had moved to the ranch, and Preston had kept with the tradition. If he knew one thing about dogs, it was that they worked hard for love and toys—but they worked extra hard for treats.

It didn't matter what kind of dog either. He had drug-sniffing dogs and people-sniffing dogs and gun-sniffing dogs—and cadaver-sniffing dogs, because *cadaver* was a fancy word for dead body.

Preacher went for the live people, mostly, although he'd let you know if there was a dead rabbit nearby. Or a dead person, but that was depressing.

Preston took in strays and tested them for aptitude, and some dogs took to people work with so much enthusiasm, Preston had to wonder if they'd been people before they were dogs. The dogs that had aptitude were trained up, but even if they were dumber than posts, Preston always had a place for them on the ranch. And if the ranch wasn't their favorite place, he had help finding them a place somewhere else.

Ozzy and his girlfriend, Belinda, had moved in with Preston after his grandmother died and his mom had moved to a nearby apartment complex. Preston had taken nearly every animal husbandry class his local junior college had to offer and was capable of giving his dogs shots, of helping the pregnant ones give birth, and of stitching up the occasional ripped ear or damaged paw. He made a small income supplying trained dogs for the local law enforcement, and he got a commission whenever he helped Glen and Damien with their private search-and-rescue business.

Preston spent six hours a week training with his local dog association, learning police protocols when dogs were being employed, networking with the other dog trainers so he and his dogs could help more than they got in the way. It was enough to pay the taxes, to keep up the house, to feed and house the dogs. At least once a month, he and the dogs he was working with most participated in an overnight exercise or endurance run—taking dogs through uninhabited land and looking for lost campers or hikers was not for the weak or the unprepared.

Training rescue dogs was no way to get rich. Preston was lucky, because Glen and Damien had gotten funding for their business and included him in it. He could afford to pay Ozzy and Belinda with more than free rent.

But the work was, in the end, a labor of love.

"What a wonderful dog," the woman behind the counter said happily. "He's a service dog?"

"Yes." Preston thought the orange vest was self-explanatory, but she seemed well-intentioned.

"What kind of service? Antianxiety? Epilepsy? Depression?"

"He finds people," Preston said, wondering if she thought Preston had those things. He smiled extra wide so she would think he was okay and not ask him any personal questions.

"Dead people?" she squeaked, and on the plus side, she suddenly looked less interested in *him*, but on the minus side, now she looked afraid.

"Live people are his specialty," he said. "But I have dogs at home who will find you super quick if you're dead and need that."

The woman held her hand to her throat, like she was afraid Preston was going to make *her* dead. He tried another smile, and she recoiled, and he lowered his hand to Preacher's head. Preacher licked his wrist, and Preston relaxed his smile. He *knew* Preacher was his friend—he had nothing to prove here.

The woman resumed ringing up the tremendous grocery order, and Preston paid for it and left.

As he was loading the car, Preacher waiting patiently at his heels, he reflected that people didn't understand the nature of dogs at all. Preston didn't bring Preacher into Walmart because he needed company or because Preacher could do something for him—he brought his buddy with him because Preston *loved* him. Dogs were so simple. You gave them a task, and you gave them a reward. Sometimes the reward was beef jerky or Pup-Peroni. Sometimes it was a solid pet and an attaboy. What the dogs didn't realize was that watching them work, giving them the task, giving them the reward—that was *Preston's* reward. Big happy furry bodies—or little wriggling yapping ones—and all of that ferocious goodwill.

Most dog handlers worked for free in their spare hours—and each dog required an amazing number of hours to train. Preston only knew of one dog handler in his association who had a functional working relationship that wasn't with dogs—and that was because Carla's wife also worked with her own dogs. It was a family thing.

Preston had gotten lots of sex in college, and that was lucky, because for the last few years, not counting a few hookups when he'd been out running rescue jobs with Glen and Damien, his great romance had been with his dogs.

Which was fine, because no lover had lived up to the torch he'd carried for Damien. He'd expected the burning in his chest whenever Damien smiled at him or went in for a hug to dim over the last twelve years. He wasn't stupid—he knew people's feelings changed over time.

But Damien had only gotten more wonderful.

Even in the last year and a half, since the accident, when all of that happy chatter stopped and Damien had looked almost afraid of his own words every time he spoke, Damien had remained wonderful.

Irritating and closed off, maybe, and he'd continued to regard Preston with a look that Preston had no corresponding picture for. He couldn't define what was wrong with Damien, and that had been hard. Damien was always so good at defining things for Preston—when he couldn't define things about himself, Preston was left cross and at sea. It had something to do with Damien's leg, and something to do with how he'd gotten sick before he flew, but Preston needed Damien to connect the dots for him, and Damien kept running away from a conversation that would do that.

Preston had asked Glen if he'd done anything wrong, but Glen's answer had been… less than satisfactory.

The previous year, in the godforsaken month of February

"WHAT did Mallory say?" Damien asked, looking pale and waxy in the hospital bed.

Glen looked up from Damien's phone and rolled his eyes. "He said the funeral was nice, and he and Tevyn are humping like bunnies."

Preston laughed, because bunnies *did* hump a lot, and after Mallory and Tevyn had been rescued from the helicopter crash that had injured Damien, they'd looked at each other like they'd wanted to hump.

"That's rude," Damien muttered. "Just rude. I don't want to know if they're humping like bunnies. I don't want to know if they're humping like turtles. I just wanted to know if they were okay."

Glen tilted his head, his eyes narrowed like he was about to say something completely shitty that nobody would forgive him for but Damien.

"They're okay, Damien. They were okay two weeks ago after the crash, and they were okay a week ago when Tevyn's grandmother died. What you really wanted to know is if Mallory has suddenly given up the sad, helpless crush he's had on Tevyn for, hello, *five years*, and decided that he'd rather hump you instead. The answer is no. Close your eyes, go to sleep, and try to forget they're ripping your leg open again tomorrow."

Damien's warm brown eyes were enormous. "Remember the last time I saved your life?"

Glen bit his lip in thought. "Bangladesh, two years ago. It was *not* my fault that guy grabbed my ass in a no-gay zone, but thank you."

"Consider it revoked. Invent a time machine, go back to that moment, and don't count on me to evac you from someone's backyard this time."

Glen let out a filthy laugh. "That guy gave great head. Totally worth it. Now shut up and sleep."

Damien opened his mouth to offer what would probably be a brutal retort, but Glen stood restlessly. "Preston, keep him from leaving. I'm going to hit the head and get us something to eat."

"Which you will eat in front of me when I get nothing but ice chips? Get back in that time machine. I'm killing you twice."

Glen's laughter was still filthy as he left, but Damien's irritated face vanished as soon as the door shut, and he tilted his head back against the pillows wearily.

"Are you in pain?" Preston asked, expecting Damien to lie like he had been for the last two weeks.

"A little," Damien said, surprising him. "I'm… happy, I guess, for my friends."

"You don't look happy," Preston said, hating the green feeling of jealousy in his chest. He'd known Damien had crushed on Mallory Armstrong since he'd begun shuttling Mallory for work, and he'd contented himself with the knowledge that Glen had been certain Mallory was in love with Tevyn. Now that they were together, seeing Damien sad… hurt.

"I am," Damien said. And then, surprisingly, continued, "That's not a lie. I'm just…." His lips twisted in what would probably have been a pretend smile.

"Tell the truth," Preston demanded. He was already tired of this Damien who lied.

"I am not feeling like a man to love," Damien replied, and that sounded like the truth, even though Preston didn't understand.

"You should be loved," Preston said, dismayed. "Why wouldn't anybody love you?"

Damien shook his head and avoided his eyes. "I'm being a dork. I'm starving, and my leg hurts, and this is the most you've talked to me since I've gotten back."

"You're hurt, and I don't know what to say," Preston replied shortly. "I don't like it when you're hurt. You come back from surgery, and you lie there, and you look dead, and I hate that. You're not supposed to be hurt, and you're not supposed to be sad, and you're not supposed to be crushing over Mallory Armstrong."

"Well, it's not like *you* want to kiss me either!" Damien snapped, and Preston blinked.

Anger washed over him, and he lied like a teenager then. "Why would I want to kiss you? You're sad."

"No reason at all," Damien muttered and turned his face away. "Go away, Preston. I need to sleep."

Preston stood up and left, hurt, but when he'd gotten outside, Glen had been there, hands full of sandwiches, face full of exasperation.

"You don't think he meant that, do you?"

Preston gaped at his older brother—not his bigger brother anymore. Preston had passed him up by four inches in his senior year of high school. Glen had a smaller, prettier face and expressive blue eyes. Preston didn't doubt he got laid all the time, but like with Damien, he didn't want details either.

"But he's *Damien*. He *never* says things he doesn't mean. Not to *me*."

"Well, you just told him you didn't want to kiss him, and I know *that's* a lie. He's hurt, Preston. And he wasn't in love with Mallory, but he was distracted by him. He needs us to be patient with him until he's back on his feet."

Preston nodded unhappily, but he regarded Glen with a great deal of faith. "Should I… should I tell him?" he asked finally. "That I've never stopped wanting to kiss him?"

Glen shrugged, uncharacteristically uncertain. "No," he said after a few moments. "No. Not yet. Wait until he can come home from the hospital, Preston. Wait until he can walk again. Wait until he can get back in the air." For the first time since Damien had been rescued, strapped to the back of a makeshift sled and wearing a helmet slapped together with chair stuffing and duct tape, Preston got to see his brother's unguarded expression, and he realized that Glen had been wearing a lying face for two weeks too.

"We almost lost him," Glen said softly. "And he knows that. And he's afraid. Men like… like Damien—

like me—we're not brave like you. We can't always tell the world what we're thinking. It hurts us sometimes. Give him time."

SO Preston had given him time.

He'd given him a year and a half, and Damien might have recovered from his crush on Mallory Armstrong, but he hadn't stopped wearing his lying face, hadn't stopped being quiet and withdrawn. The last time Preston had heard Damien threaten Glen with death had been in that hospital room, and Preston was done.

Preston was determined that Damien had gotten all the time he was going to get, and they were going to start discussing why they hadn't kissed yet.

It was almost as important as getting his brother back.

When Preston got back to the hangar, Damien had pulled the Cessna out to the tarmac and was busy positioning the supplies they did have to make way for what Preston had bought behind the cargo net. They loaded up quickly, making room for Preacher to lie down behind Damien so Preston could reach out and pet him if he needed, and setting their essentials in two backpacks in the seat behind Preston's. Preston had brought a charged tablet full of games that he used to help settle his mind, and a charger to go with it, because when the tablet went out and he was in a strange place, staying centered got a lot harder. He'd also brought sudoku books, because those helped when the tablet failed, but not too many because they were bulky.

Damien pulled the hangar door closed and locked up, then got into the pilot's seat, his body moving with that steady confidence Preston had always associated with him. Even with the limp, for a moment, it was easy to pretend nothing had changed.

Preston was silent as Damien radioed the control tower of the little airstrip and then taxied to the takeoff. He remembered when Damien and Glen would sit in the front and talk bullshit from the minute they got into the plane to the minute one of them would leave the other in charge and cop a nap in the back.

Damien didn't talk bullshit anymore—he clenched his teeth and squared his jaw and tackled every takeoff and landing like it was the most serious thing in the entire world.

It was unnatural. It was like if one day, Preacher stopped being Preston's best friend and became a burden on him instead.

Preacher was never a burden. Preston knew that dogs lived shorter lives than humans—he'd said goodbye to several dogs he'd loved with all his heart. His grandma had told him that the shorter lifespan was God's way of making people pay attention to dogs, because otherwise they took them for granted. Preston never took his dogs for granted—and seeing Damien hate the thing he'd loved so much made his chest hollow and achy.

It needed to stop.

Preston waited until Damien had reached cruising height and the plane had leveled off in its flight toward LA before he broached the subject.

Turbulence

DAMIEN took a deep breath and turned his head, the better to see if Preston was really serious about this subject at this moment.

"Really? You're going to ask me about this now?"

Preston was, of course, unruffled. "I told you we'd talk about it. Why are you surprised?"

"Because!" Damien looked back at the clear sky, trying to find peace in the wide-open blue. For a moment it worked, but then he was taken back to when God had apparently decided to crumple his helicopter in one casual gesture and tossed it into the middle of the Sierra winter.

He was prepared for the sudden jerk of his breathing, because it happened every time he flew now, but he wasn't sure if he could hide it from—

"I saw that," Preston said. God, he was persistent. His eyebrows drew down, his mouth compressed, and his entire face tightened. Damien just wanted to rub his thumbs over all those fearsome forehead wrinkles and soothe them away, but he couldn't do that when Preston was aiming all of that terrifying will *at Damien*. "I saw that, but…." And for once Preston didn't sound sure of himself. "I don't know what it means. Let's start with that. What does that look mean?"

"I'm not sure being up in the air is the best time to talk about this," Damien said, his own uncertainty very much to the fore. He'd been shoving all of this fear back down his gullet for the last year—ever since he'd gotten back in the air—and he wasn't sure when it was worse. When he was up in the air, he very much had to do things to keep him that way. If he could cling to the gears, to the stick, with enough ferocity, if he could exert *every ounce of his will* on the aircraft, it might not go down.

Might.

That "might" was the only thing that got him on the plane sometimes.

"Well, you won't let me talk about it any other time," Preston said. Preston was nothing if not logical. "If you'd talked to me down on the ground, we wouldn't be having this conversation now."

"Maybe I don't want to have this conversation at all," Damien snarked. "Maybe we could be talking about movies!"

"Fine," Preston said. "Let's talk about the movie where the two guys who should be having sex are having a conversation in an airplane."

"I haven't seen that one," Damien said dryly. "Does the airplane land?"

"Safely," Preston said, completely serious. "Like airplanes do ninety-nine percent of the time."

"Yeah, but it's that one percent that'll kill ya." Damien felt his lips twisting. Preston was not particularly good at sparring—not like Glen, who would exchange barbs with him until their mouths dried up and their tongues fell out. But when Preston *did* fire back, the results were often hilarious—and always 100 percent truthful.

"This one won't." Preston's cheerful confidence was Damien's undoing.

"How do you know?" he asked, and he'd meant to keep things light, to effectively avoid the conversation Preston had been pushing for, but the throbbing in his voice was something not even Preston could miss.

"Because you have to believe that, don't you?" Preston asked. "It's how you and my brother take off and land almost every day."

Damien's next breath was shakier than he would have liked. "But it only takes once," he said. He wanted to look at something, anything, but he was *flying a plane*. He had to look at gauges—that reminded him sometimes gauges lied. He had to look at the sky, clear and blue and cloudless, but you couldn't see turbulence, could you? He had to look at—

Preston's hand on his shoulder was unexpected, and Damien's eyes flew over to meet his, startled. Preston made direct eye contact, which didn't happen often, and only with family, before *Damien* had to look away.

"I was worried about Glen," Preston said.

The blood hummed under Damien's skin like the eye contact had been hands on his body. "Now?"

"Well, yes, now—but when he first went into the Air Force to be a pilot. Our mother was furious—all the good grades, all the charm." Preston swallowed. "He was so good with people." As Preston was not. Damien could hear the unspoken part of that. "I didn't want my brother to die."

"He didn't," Damien soothed.

"And we met you, and I didn't want *you* to die."

Damien swallowed. It had been a near thing. "I'm sorry I scared you," he said gruffly.

"But everybody dies. You can't stop it. You can just have the happiest life you can manage."

"It's what I've always believed," Damien said, cheered up a little hearing it from Preston's mouth.

"Then why are you doing this?" Preston asked, his voice rising one of the few times of their friendship.

"Because we need to get to Glen!" Damien shouted back.

"You're being dense! That's not my question, and you know it!"

Damien found a surprised smile twisting his lips. "What question are you asking, again? I'll be honest, Preston, I'm lost."

Preston scowled at him. "I'm asking why you get sick before you fly now. Why does your sweat smell funny? What's wrong? Your leg isn't all of it. *What's wrong*?"

Maybe it was the repeated question or the worry about Glen. Maybe it was the fact that Preston was sitting so close—so close Damien could feel his body heat, smell that wholesome combination of dogs and hay and sun and sweat. Maybe it was that the hug Preston had given had been solid and real and life affirming.

But Damien said it, the thing he hadn't even wanted to say to Glen in the last year and a half, even though they all knew it was the truth. "I'm afraid."

Preston let out a long breath. "Why now? Why not when you were deployed?"

Damien blew out a breath of his own. He and Glen had been forced into more than one emergency landing—even one or two that could be considered crashes, although Glen had always maintained that if it didn't get him sent Stateside, it wasn't a crash and they didn't need to tell his mom.

But this….

Damien kept his hands locked on the wheel, but his mind wandered back.

"The winds were brutal," he said thoughtfully. "We knew that." Tevyn's grandmother had been dying, and Damien's job had been to fly them from a snowboarding event near Donner Pass back down to San Francisco. Tev and Mallory had still told him to use his good judgment—they'd trusted him to know when to call it—and he'd thought he'd been okay.

"Thirty knots, which is pretty bad, but the rule of thumb is to call it at forty. I'd looked at the weather charts—said it got to about thirty-five but should have still been clear. And then, right when we were naked, no place to land, this big, wild gust of wind slammed into me at forty-five knots. I'd just swung around to take us back—I didn't like the way the trees were moving, didn't like the feel of the bird, and… *bam*! It was like the hand of God, picking us up and slamming us against the snow."

His voice shook, and he had to blink hard and fast to keep his vision in front of him.

You have to land this plane, dumbass. Why the fuck would you open that wound and bleed out when you still have to land the goddamned plane?

"I would have been scared," Preston said, and Damien risked a glance at him.

He was staring at Damien's profile hungrily, like hearing this story fed his soul—and he waited until the last moment to skitter his eyes toward Damien's right ear. How had Damien missed how much Preston had needed this moment, this explanation, this contact?

"I wasn't," Damien said, which was the truth but surprising at the same time. "I was shocked. And then I was in—" He shuddered. "—so much pain. Mal and Tevyn had to give me a field dressing in the snow so I wouldn't bleed out. Tevyn almost died getting the first aid kit and his go-bag from the chopper—it was about to go over the cliff. If he hadn't done that, we all would have been dead."

"Tevyn left first," Preston said, which was true. Tevyn had stayed long enough to see Damien out of his second surgery, but he'd been on a plane soon after.

"His grandmother was dying," Damien reminded him. "He had to say goodbye."

"Mallory left the day after." This seemed to be a grudge.

"He made sure I was stable after the third surgery." Damien remembered that. He'd opened his eyes and Mallory had been there, kind and worried. He and Mal had been friends, both of them nursing their hopeless crushes on younger men. Watching Mallory and Tevyn discover that their love for each other was real and wonderful—and not painful at all, in spite of what Preston thought—had been one of the things that had kept Damien alive on that mountaintop when every breath had been pain.

"He shouldn't have left!"

Ah, Preston. Loyal—fiercely, fiercely loyal. Even this past year when Damien had done everything but wear a T-shirt that read "GTFO!" he should have known that Preston wouldn't desert him.

"He and Tevyn stayed with me on the mountain," Damien explained. "They got me down, to help. Don't you understand? They thought it was okay because they were leaving me with you." *How was I supposed to know you really didn't want me?*

"But you didn't want us," Preston said bitterly. "Or you didn't want *me*."

Damien took a deep breath, and Preston grunted.

"That's a lying breath," Preston told him, and Damien's temper pricked.

"Oh, how would you know! I've never lied to you!"

"You're about to lie right now! You're about to say you *do* want me and Glen for family, but that's not true, because if it was true, how come you don't talk to us, and *how come we're not having sex*?"

"*Because why would you want to have sex with a coward who can barely walk!*"

Damien *really* wished he could see Preston's face at that moment, because the series of expressions that crossed it in profile was both fascinating and frightening.

Finally, Preston asked, "Are you talking about *you*?"

Damien shook his head and sank into his shoulders, and his face compressed into the scowl that seemed to define him since he'd realized his leg would *always* hurt, would *never* be 100 percent, and he'd never again be the guy Preston had followed with hero worship in his eyes.

"You know anyone else who's afraid to fly? Who can't seem to push past the pincushion in his leg?"

"You walk fine," Preston snapped. "I'm sorry it hurts. Maybe if you let me rub it, it wouldn't hurt so much!"

"It's hideous," Damien muttered. Scar tissue twisted across the leg from midcalf practically to his hip. His femur had popped through his skin—Tevyn had needed to reset it on the mountainside or Damien would have bled out. But the result had been imperfect healing and an infection that had raged long after they'd gotten Damien back to civilization. "Why would you even want to touch it?"

"*Because it's your skin!*"

Preston's holler rebounded through Damien's skull. "Jesus, Preston—"

"Don't tell me to use my inside voice!" Preston yelled. "I'm tired of inside voice! You were hurt—I can help. Don't be stubborn!"

"Why do you even want to have sex with a man you feel sorry for?" Damien yelled back. He wasn't going to hold back if Preston wasn't. "Jesus, Preston, do you think I want us to start a grown-up relationship when it's all 'Oh, poor Damien, he hasn't been the same since the accident.' *I wanted to be perfect* before I tried to kiss my best friend's little brother. Did that ever occur to you?"

"You were never perfect," Preston told him crossly. "You and Glen and all those fuckin' words. I used to ask Glen, 'Why do you guys have to talk so much?' and Glen would say, 'We like making each other laugh,' so that was fine. If it made you happy, I could deal with all the words, but you were *not* perfect before the crash. *That* is a *lie.*"

"Well, why would you want to kiss me if there were too many goddamned words?" Damien asked. Great—wasn't perfect before the crash, sure wasn't perfect after it. Why were they having this conversation again?

"Because you're Damien," Preston muttered, crossing his arms and staring out the window on his side of the plane.

Clouds and sky—Damien's favorite view, actually—but he could see how it would get boring. "There's got to be more to it than that," Damien said, scanning the sky for something, anything, to guide him through this particular moment in time.

"Why?" Preston asked. "Isn't it enough that I want to kiss you?"

Damien opened his mouth, struggling for the words Preston had accused him of having too many of. Nobody was more surprised than he was when Preston came up with some first.

"Don't *you* want to kiss me?" Preston asked, and the plaintive note in his voice undid Damien.

"So much," Damien said gruffly. "So much. Since your grandmother's funeral, remember?"

"I remember," Preston said, hurt saturating the moment. "Your eyes were the color of a dark sun."

"Yours were the color of a cloudless sky."

Preston's hand on his knee was warm and knowing, and in spite of himself, Damien was drawn back to that day and how much he'd wanted to comfort Preston, and how, for the first time, he wasn't sure whether Preston would welcome his hug.

Five years ago

DAMIEN had to hand it to Preston's grandmother. She hadn't kicked it quietly, or in bed. She'd gone off on a long training weekend with her dog-handling group and had suffered a massive myocardial infarction two hours from the nearest transportation.

It wouldn't have mattered. She'd died quickly and with no suffering, surrounded by the snuffling, furry, kind population she'd loved the best during her life. Everybody had agreed it hadn't been a bad way to go.

But that didn't mean Preston and Glen, who had been partially raised by their grandmother after their father had taken off, hadn't mourned her with all their hearts.

The day of the wake—held at the ranch, where her fellow dog handlers could bring their comfort companions—Glen had been consoling his mother, and Damien had looked around and realized Preston had disappeared.

"You know where he is, right?"

Ozzy was five feet seven inches of stocky goodwill. He had a broad face that still bore the scars of a vicious bout of adolescent acne, and a smile that would illumine the heavens. His girlfriend, Belinda, was a curvy blond goddess who looked at Ozzy like he held the sun and the moon and the stars in his broad, capable hands, and Damien reflected—not for the first time—that Preston's long-ago desire to kiss his best friend came from all the good things in Preston's soul.

"Yeah, I know." Damien grimaced. "How's he doing?"

Ozzy shrugged. "Asked me and Belinda to move in almost before the funeral was finalized. But then, he's wanted that for a long time, and Lavinia was...." Ozzy trailed off. Lavinia had been a good woman, but in her own way, she was as stubborn as Preston.

"She didn't like most people," Damien said diplomatically. Damien had arrived under Glen's umbrella, and Glen, glib, charming, irritating as fuck Glen, had managed it somehow.

"Nope. But Preston needs the help." Ozzy smiled conspiratorially. "He's already got business contacts at the police station for helping to train their police dogs, and he's working on his certification to train service dogs for children with autism." He tapped his forehead. "Our boy is forward thinking. And seriously, Bel and I can't imagine a better life than spending all day with dogs."

Damien had laughed, because he got to live *his* dream too, and fly all over creation, which was all he'd ever wanted to do. Preston surrounded himself with good people. That made Damien happy.

"I'll go find him," he said. "Make sure he's okay."

"Here." Ozzy reached into his good Sunday suit and pulled out a handful of dog treats. "Patsy's got her hands full with that litter. She could always use a little more fat."

Damien took the treats and tucked them into the pocket of *his* Sunday best, then slipped out of the somber room of desperately uncomfortable dog handlers who would rather be mourning with their best friends.

The dogs spent a lot of time running around, but giant dog packs were dangerous unchecked. Preston kept most of the dogs kenneled when they weren't being worked, and between him, Ozzy, and Belinda, every dog got plenty of time out of the kennels with lots of exercise. The little ones had three different kennels between them, with a small crate for each small dog— every dog had a safe space.

That was Preston's rule.

Glen had told him once that Preston had spent a lot of his childhood voluntarily in the closet because it made him feel safer. Their father yelled a lot, not necessarily at the boys but in general, and Preston would simply… sit in the closet and pet the family dog. When they'd gone to live with their grandmother, when Preston was six, sitting in one of the kennels with the dog that seemed to need the most attention was Preston's best thing.

Patsy, a Heinz-57 pit bull mix, had just given birth to seven puppies. The biggest, a moose-baby with enormously broad feet and a head like a beach ball made of brick, liked to sit still and watch all the other puppies crawl over one another and be cute. Glen had called the dog "Preacher" because he looked like he was giving words of wisdom to the masses, and Preston had already made plans to keep this one for himself when the others were weaned.

Damien had no doubt whatsoever where he'd find Preston.

Because Patsy had a growing family, the kennel was mostly a big wooden box with an open side, surrounded by chain-link fence. Preston and company spent a good two hours a day picking up dog crap, so the dirt floor to the box was only that—dirt—and Patsy and her babies had a giant burlap pillow to keep warm and comfy on.

The box was barely big enough to house Patsy, her nursing family, and one grown man sitting cross-legged in the back corner.

After Damien joined Preston, it housed two of them.

It was raining that day, which didn't happen that often in Napa, and it seemed the weather mourned the old woman who had loved living so much of her life out in it. Damien was grateful for the clean dry straw in the box and the shelter from the rain.

They sat side by side for a few moments until Preacher finished eating and crawled into Preston's lap. Preston grunted and spent some time running his hands over the broad head and the silkiness of the triangular ears and the precious little toe-beans of the paws. Preacher dragged his long tongue over any exposed part of Preston he could find.

Damien was surprised when Preston broke the silence.

"Gran hated rain."

"She did indeed."

"She was so excited about that trip. Twenty-four hours to find their target and come back—she'd been practicing all year."

"I know. Handling the dogs was her best thing besides you and your brother." The relationship between Preston's grandmother and Preston's mother had always been strained. Damien got the feeling that the older woman had been a lot like Preston—nuance and expression were not always her forte—but that hadn't stopped her from giving the boys everything in her power to have a happy childhood.

Who could wish for a better childhood than one surrounded by dogs?

"She was so good at being quiet," Preston said mournfully. "Nobody else will be that kind of quiet."

It was on the tip of Damien's tongue to say he could be, but he stopped himself because Preston didn't like lying.

"No, but you will have other kinds of quiet in your life," Damien said. "And some noise too. Me and Glen will bring the noise, Ozzy and Belinda will bring the kindness, and you will find a nice guy to bring the quiet."

Preston's rolled eyes could have meant several things, but his words were quite succinct. "God, you're dumb."

Damien recoiled in hurt. "Right. Sorry—I'll leave now." He put his hands down to crawl out of the crate, but Preston's hand on his wrist stopped him.

"I don't want you to go!"

"But you just said I was dumb! Seriously, Preston, it's okay if you want to be alone. I mean, I thought you might need comforting, but not everybody does. If you want me to leave, I'll—"

"That's not why you're dumb. Of course I want you with me. I always want you with me."

Damien rocked backward and into his sitting position again. "Okay," he said. "I give. Why am I dumb?"

"Because I don't want another guy to bring the quiet! I don't care about quiet with guys."

"Then what do you want?" The question was sincere, but the crate was close and warm, and Preston smelled like warm, slightly sweating man, a little bit of aftershave, and dogs.

He smelled like comfort, and while he kept his eyes on Preacher, he kept flickering his gaze to Damien's face and back, and Damien was wondering what he was looking for.

"I want you," Preston said, and Damien blinked because that could mean several things.

Damien thought he knew what it meant. "I'm going to put my arm around your shoulder, buddy. Don't startle."

Preston leaned into him, and Damien closed his eyes for a moment, not wanting to pretend that this was any more intimate than Preston thought it was—but dammit, wanting Preston right there next to him so badly. He'd loved Lavinia too. She'd welcomed him to the ranch twice a year, no questions, no explanations. Just like Preston, she was kind to creatures who needed it but didn't really have a place for any person who didn't take the time to understand her.

Preston turned toward him, and for a moment their eyes met. "I want to kiss you now," Preston said. "Do you consent?"

Damien recoiled, dropping his arm. "No!" His body screamed *Yes!* But he was trying to be a good guy.

Preston pulled back, thumping against their little shelter with a muttered oath. "I thought you liked me!"

"I do!"

"Why are you sitting here with your arm around me if you don't like me in the kissing way!"

"I'm trying to comfort you!" Damien snapped. "I needed comfort. I was trying to... I don't know, comfort us both!"

"So was I!" Preston yelled. Patsy gave a growl, because no dog likes that much emotion near her babies, and Preston lowered his voice. "I think sex would make me *very* happy right now!"

Damien gave a strangled laugh. "Sex makes everybody happy *right now*," he said. "But it doesn't necessarily make people happy *later*. I... I like you, Preston. I want to keep being with you as Glen's brother. Sex might mess that up."

Preston glared at him, eyes red-rimmed, forehead creased. "Would you want to be with me if I *wasn't* Glen's brother?" he asked suspiciously.

"Why, are you thinking of killing Glen in his sleep?" The snark snuck out, and for a moment Damien held his breath, hoping Preston would see the joke.

Well, yes and no.

"I know you said that to be funny, but I don't get it," Preston told him unhappily. "Is *that* why you won't kiss me? Because I don't get your jokes?"

Damien's heart broke a little. "You are handsome," he said, smiling faintly, because it was an understatement. Preston was *beautiful*. "And you are kind. And…." His body tingled from being there. "My body wants you."

"But your mind doesn't? Or your heart? Or whatever it is people say wants somebody but doesn't?"

"No," Damien told him crossly. "All those things want you. But don't you get it? Your grandmother just died, and I'm one of the solid people in your life. Lovers don't always stay, Preston. Do you really want to risk that between us?" He thought of his parents in Hawaii, his mother desperately trying to make peace between him and his father, his father bitter and taciturn because Damien threw away what he'd thought of as a promising future in business.

"No," Preston admitted, sounding miserable.

"I don't either," Damien told him. "You and your brother are my best family."

Preston let out a strangled little sob. "You can put your arm around my shoulder again," he said, sounding defeated. "Just… just tell me, okay?"

"Tell you what?"

"When I can kiss you. I've waited for a long time already."

Damien closed his eyes and pulled him closer. "Wait until you're not grieving," he said. "Wait until it's all okay."

For once, Preston didn't ask the obvious question. What did he mean, "all okay"? But Damien was relieved, because he didn't have an answer for that. He and Glen had exited the military the month before, and Gecko Inc. was but a seed in Glen's brain at that point. Lavinia was gone, and they were both worried about Preston.

And Damien hadn't had a relationship that lasted longer than a year, and he didn't want to risk that with Preston.

Preston was too dear, too important to muddy up their relationship with sex. Besides, what would Damien tell Glen?

Now

PRESTON squeezed that warm hand on Damien's knee, and Damien shuddered and covered it with his own.

"Are you cold?" Preston asked, but there was a mocking edge to his voice that told Damien he knew exactly what he was doing.

"No," Damien said grumpily.

"Am I touching the part that hurts?"

Damien was tempted to say yes, but Preston would feel bad, and that wouldn't be fair. "Your hand feels really good. It's been a...."

"Finish the sentence." And that mocking edge was still there.

"It's been a long time since I was touched," Damien muttered. God, the best and worst thing about communicating with Preston was that you couldn't evade and you couldn't play word games. Damien would normally use this moment as an excuse to flirt— *"It's a good thing I'm not ticklish!"* or *"The arm rest not good enough for you?"*

But not with Preston, and Preston knew it.

"We could have been touching," Preston said cheerfully. He moved his hand up higher on Damien's thigh. "We could have been touching for the last five years."

"Yeah, but I didn't even have my act together five years ago. We didn't put the business together until a few months after that. And why would you want to touch me now?"

Preston moved his hand from Damien's thigh to Preacher's head, where it rested on the seat behind them.

"I am still not understanding what the problem is," Preston mumbled. "Why am I having such a hard time with this?" He turned to Damien accusingly. "*You*," he said in irritation, "aren't making any sense. Why would I not want to touch you now? Because you're afraid?"

"It's not very attractive in a man, is it?" Damien shot back.

"But if we're going to be kissing, wouldn't it be my job to make you feel better?"

"Lovers fall down on that job all the time," Damien muttered. The truth was, he hadn't had any lovers since the crash. The one thing he'd thought about when he'd been up on that mountain was coming back and telling Preston how he felt—how he'd felt for the longest time—that he agreed. They *should* be kissing.

But Preston's seeming rejection—and his own body's treacherous lack of healing—had persuaded him that maybe they shouldn't.

He didn't think he could take Preston's revulsion if he saw Damien's leg now.

"I wouldn't," Preston told him. "I know you go up in the air every day when you're afraid—that's brave. I broke my wrist riding a horse in high school, remember?"

"Glen read your letter to our barracks," Damien said, not wanting to smile. Preston's version of the horse that made no goddamned sense had been highly entertaining. Damien had grown up around the animals—had, in fact, played polo during his high school years—and he'd known exactly what Preston had been doing wrong. He'd felt for both of them, the confused human and the *very* confused horse.

"I've never gone back on a horse," Preston told him. "I figured me and horses were just not meant to be, or I'd understand them like I understand dogs. And you could have done that with flying. Decided that you and helicopters or you and planes just weren't meant to be. But you didn't. You've been trying to get back that part of you that loved it—and that's amazing."

Preston moved the hand back, and Damien realized his knee felt naked without it. "It's not amazing," he said bitterly. "I'm… it still scares me." And yet that got a little easier to say.

"It's amazing to *me*," Preston said, his voice a little wobbly. "Does that mean something to you? Personally? Because it's me?"

Damien found himself threading their fingers together. "Yeah. Yeah, that means a lot to me. I… I like being your hero," he admitted.

"I'd rather be your lover," Preston told him, and maybe because he didn't say *kissing* or *sex*, so baldly that part of Damien flinched, this sank in.

For a few moments he flew in silence, searching for words, but he kept tight hold of Preston's hand.

"You're done talking now," Preston said, and all Damien could do was nod.

Nayarit

PRESTON had spent the night before they left worried about Glen and unable to sleep. He'd known that he and Damien would be flying out the next morning, so he'd gone around to all the dog kennels, said hi to his friends, made sure everybody was happy, fed, watered, and healthy, and had then sat down and done the books and written out training plans for Ozzy and Belinda.

Ozzy and Belinda were smart about the animals, and they listened to Preston closely because he had the degree in animal husbandry, but writing the training plans and nutrition requirements for everybody helped Preston organize things in his head, and they never questioned it. Besides, Ozzy told Preston privately that Belinda's attention span wasn't that great—she had trouble organizing things in her head—and the lists really helped her do a good job.

She'd been told her whole life that she was pretty, but she really only felt smart at Preston's place, where they could take care of dogs and make them happy.

But just putting things in order with the ranch made it easier for Preston to sleep now. His mind wasn't going back and forth trying to remember what he'd forgotten.

And Damien was holding his hand.

The touch was such a relief. It felt honest, like a promise. Like there would be hugging later.

And kissing.

And sex.

Ever since Preston had become sexually active, he'd thought about Damien, his kind brown eyes, his smile.

Damien would probably laugh a lot during sex—he'd probably crack jokes and say nervous things until Preston took over his mouth in one of several ways he'd learned.

Dreaming about making Damien quiet and having his body respond to Preston's was enough to send a tingle under Preston's skin.

So much about Damien was appealing. Preston was fascinated by his mouth, because it was that perfect medium between full and lean. By his hair, which was black and thick and wavy. By his hands, which were amazingly long-fingered and gentle. Preston had seen him giving bottles to puppies on the ranch, and he'd touched them so delicately.

Preston knew Damien's leg would be scarred and imperfect. He was wearing jeans today—when he normally would be wearing cargo shorts, because it was hot and they were more practical. Preston knew enough about how people were embarrassed to know that Damien had stopped wearing shorts after the accident for a reason.

He just didn't think Damien would specifically want to hide his leg from *Preston*. But the more they talked, the more Preston realized that Damien had really wanted to kiss Preston as much as Preston wanted to kiss Damien. He realized that maybe Damien was *more* embarrassed in front of Preston.

Damien wanted Preston to think well of him.

Complicated.

Emotions were complicated. Glen told him once that emotions were like a pile of tiny puppies, all of them wiggling toward one goal. Sorting them out required care, because if you pulled on a tail thinking it led to one puppy but you accidentally pulled too hard, you would hurt someone who was only trying to find comfort.

Preston didn't want to tweak Damien's tail, but he would *really* like to single him out of all the other puppies so Damien could be his and his alone.

And maybe forcing him to talk while they'd been in the air had been necessary, like tweaking a tail to find the right puppy was sometimes.

But all of that sorting, that peopling, that forcing Damien to communicate clearly—it was all exhausting, and Preston fell asleep, hard and deeply, in the front of the airplane.

When he woke up, Damien had untangled their fingers and was radioing a control tower for permission to land and refuel outside of Los Angeles. Preston reached back for Preacher to touch his head instinctively as they circled the airfield and began a gentle descent. Preston had never claimed to be good at flying—he'd never gotten the hang of landing without nervousness. When he had to fly commercial, he would listen to music with his eyes closed for the last half of the trip so he didn't have to know they were landing until the plane touched the ground.

There was a bump, and Damien pulled up the flaps to slow the vehicle down, a harsh panting sound coming from his throat. After the plane was down and taxiing toward the fuel pump, Preston opened his eyes and looked at the man next to him.

Damien's skin was normally a sort of tawny gold, but he looked almost gray now, and there were big wet stains under his arms.

Hesitantly, because he didn't want to distract him, Preston put a gentle hand on his knee.

"We're fine," he said, his voice so unnaturally loud that Preacher gave a small surprised *woof.* "You did great."

Damien's breathing evened out, and he gave Preston a wry smile before assuming the stoic death mask he apparently now wore when he was landing.

"Thanks," he said. And then he added, "Tips welcome, and be sure to tell my boss."

Preston didn't get the joke—because Damien and Glen were their *own* bosses, they owned the company!—but it *was* a joke, and it was good to hear Damien try to make one. His smile spread ear to ear and didn't fade until they'd disembarked and he was walking Preacher behind the hangars so he could take a crap.

HE got in a good jog with Preacher after the hound had taken care of business, so he was pleasantly tired and ready for the lunch Damien had bought him at the commissary. They ate at a little picnic table by the far hangar, while a mechanic checked the coolant levels and the air filters in the Cessna.

There was lots of dust in the summer, and an overheated engine was no joke at ten thousand feet up. Damien had already checked these things back in Napa—Preston had seen him finishing up when he'd returned from the store—but Preston figured Damien was allowed a little paranoia after his crash.

"Cookies!" Preston said happily, looking at the little paper packet of three that was in his meal box. Belinda was always worried about her weight, which Preston didn't understand because Ozzy thought she was beautiful, and why would she worry? But she was the one who bought groceries, and she never bought dessert.

Preston and Ozzy would take their best dogs on long hunts, sometimes, just so they could buy chocolate or ice cream at the little gas station three miles down the road.

"Belinda still on a diet?" Damien asked, chewing determinedly on his roast beef sandwich. "Because that's a shame." He'd changed his shirt since the landing, and Preston wondered if he didn't just pack extra every time he traveled. *That* would be a pain in the ass.

"I miss cookies," Preston said glumly. "Ozzy does too." He bit his lip and wondered if Ozzy would forgive him for sharing personal information. "Belinda wants to get pregnant. She says losing weight would be better for her and the baby."

But Damien's smile made the minor breach in protocol worth it. "That's wonderful! They'll be awesome parents." He frowned for a moment, like he was doing calculations in his head. "The house is big enough, right?"

"More than big enough. But there's that little cottage behind it—one big bedroom, one big living room, kitchen, bath." He smiled a little. "It's more like a *house*. But I thought I'd move in there. It would be my summer project. And then Ozzy and Belinda could have the house, and they could have lots of children to play with the puppies."

"That sounds amazing," Damien said happily. "I can't think of a better way to grow up."

A question occurred to Preston—a personal one, which didn't happen often. "Did *you* have puppies when you were growing up?"

"No," Damien said, voice dropping. "No, my parents were allergic. And even if they hadn't been, our house wasn't really dog friendly."

Preston could feel his forehead folding. "But if it's not dog friendly, it's not really kid friendly, is it?"

"Not so much," Damien said, a corner of his mouth pulling up in what should have been a smile. Damien and Glen had a whole bunch of "should have" expressions like that. Expressions that said that while their words said one thing, there were other things going on behind them.

"What is that look?" Preston asked baldly. "Why do you have that look on your face?"

"Nothing important. Kim is done with the plane. We should go." He stood up and threw away his rubbish and held out his hand for Preston's.

Preston yanked his back like a kid. "Not until you tell me what that look was."

Damien scowled. "We can't do this every time—"

"Yes, we can."

"No, we can't. We don't have time! We need to get your brother—"

"Then just tell me what that look was!"

"I was sad, okay? Because my childhood was all grades and sports and making sure I didn't track dirt through the house, and not a lot of pets and hugs. My parents buy new furniture every year and make sure nobody ever sits down on it so it's perfect. They let me get a betta fish once, but flushed it when it got a little bit pale and didn't match the rocks in the bottom of the bowl. I *love* that Ozzy and Belinda get to raise their baby on your ranch, with all the dogs in the world and parents who will hold them and play with them and an Uncle Preston who will teach them how important quiet is. Are you good now? Do you know what I'm thinking? Can we go?"

Preston regarded him in surprise. "Yes. You're right. It's getting late if we want to get to Nayarit and then go find Glen." He stood and threw away his own trash before making sure he had a firm grip on Preacher's lead—and only then realized his hands were shaking.

They walked side by side to the plane for a few strides, and then he found he had something to say after all.

"You could spend time at the ranch, with the dogs and the mess and the baby. And me. Even if we don't kiss. You know that, right?"

But Damien only grunted without answering, and Preston figured that no, it was probably news to him.

DAMIEN didn't get sick before taking off this time— Preston made careful note. But when they got in the air, he did make a request.

"Can we… you know. Not talk about hard stuff now? I'll be honest, Preston. I'm done with the hard stuff for a while."

"One more question," Preston said, thinking this should be easy.

"One. Promise?"

"Yes—it's not even that big a deal."

"Sure it's not." Even Preston understood the reversed meaning there. "Okay, shoot."

"When are you going to wear shorts again?"

Damien grunted. "When my leg doesn't look like something from a horror movie. Are we good?"

"No."

"Why am I not surprised?"

"Because you're not making any sense. It can't look like something from a horror movie when it's *your leg*."

"Two hundred and seventy-three."

"What's that number?"

"The number of stitches it took to put it back together after all the surgeries. Fourteen."

"What's that one?"

"The number of pins they had to stick in it in various places. Nine."

"I know that one," Preston said, the thought making him surly. "It's how many operations you had, total."

"Yes, and two of those were to scrape out infection in the bone."

Preston's least favorite two, because Damien had been really sick and in a lot of pain before those operations. Before the last one, he'd suggested that maybe they might want to leave him under the anesthetic, and the thought had haunted Preston ever since.

"I remember," he said.

"How's this number—ninety-seven."

"The number of days you were in the hospital," Preston answered, still cross. "I know these things. They hurt you and made me mad. And they tore apart your poor leg and put it back together again and again. It's not going to look the same, Damien. But it's still your leg. I'm going to see it when we're naked anyway."

"What makes you think we're going to be naked?" Damien snapped, sounding as surly as Preston felt. "What about any of these horrible, painful conversations indicates foreplay to you?"

Preston rolled his eyes, because the jig was up on this one. "You said you wanted me. And I want you.

And we'll be careful of each other's feelings. That's really all we need."

Damien opened and closed his mouth, and checked all his gauges in the same automatic way that Preston reached for Preacher's head. Preston waited, all patience, to see what argument Damien had to that. He needed to hear it now so he could reason his way through it before they found Glen, and he and Damien could renegotiate the terms of being him and Damien.

"Maybe you won't like kissing me," Damien said after a few moments that *he* apparently found uncomfortable but Preston was perfectly content with.

And *that* was the funniest thing he'd ever heard. Preston laughed, freely and happily, finally convinced he'd gotten the joke.

THEY came in for a landing in the state of Nayarit, near a tiny town called Las Varas. The land in this area was mostly arable, and the climate was easing into the tropical weather of Jalisco. Just humid enough to drive Preston bugshit. When Preston asked why they weren't landing in the state of Jalisco itself, Damien said there were a couple of reasons.

The first was that the area had just suffered an earthquake—most of the airports, even the private ones, were taken up with planes bringing supplies and aid to the population, and since he hadn't been invited, he didn't want to get in the way of rescue operations that had already been organized.

The second was that Glen had landed the helicopter on Buddy's strip in Las Varas, and sure enough, they could see it to the side of the one hangar in the teeny, privately owned airport as they landed. Buddy owned the landing strip and knew pretty much everything that went on in his little corner of the world.

The third reason was that Glen's satellite phone had indicated he'd been heading toward Jalisco, but over the mountains and inland—which, according to Damien, was a crazy goddamned thing to do.

"There's nothing there!" he complained. "A couple of outlying towns and farmsteads before you hit the mountains. And some seriously shitty terrain. It's a long goddamned way to get to Guadalajara or Lake Chapala is what it is, and I don't know why he'd go there!"

"Well, maybe the person he was sent to fetch wanted to go there," Preston said. "Glen's not the only one who matters."

Damien's eyes went narrow, and he stared at Preston like he was trying to fathom if Preston meant something or not.

Preston stared back at him guilelessly, thinking that if Damien didn't realize he was talking about both Damien and Glen, Damien was avoiding his point on purpose.

"Are you trying to make me crazy?" Damien asked with deep suspicion, and Preston thought about it.

"No. I don't want you *crazy*. I want you to *agree with me*. They're not the same thing, Damien."

"I wouldn't be too sure about that," Damien muttered, and then he picked up the radio and called in to Buddy at the control tower, and Preston didn't get to ask him what he meant.

The plane touched down, not quite as smoothly as last time, but Damien was scowling and moving his mouth like he was practicing what he wanted to say to Preston at some time in the future. This cheered Preston greatly—it was almost like Damien's old landings, where the plane fishtailed a little because Damien was so excited to get to where they were going so he could get up in the air again.

Once they landed, Preston and Preacher got out to do their thing, and Damien walked toward the squat little building with the twelve satellite dishes that served as the control tower.

"I'm going to talk to Buddy," he muttered. "Don't go far. And remember, Buddy keeps his horses in the west field, so maybe don't wander over there."

This was a private airfield. Preston had landed here with Glen and Damien before when they'd looked for that missing hiker who'd twisted his ankle in the mountains. He remembered, but he didn't understand. The pastures he got—open pastureland made up 80 percent of his own land, with little copses of trees by the irrigation ditch and the buildings making up the other 20 percent, and it was the same here. The terrain was a little hotter and a little more humid than Napa, but that just meant the grass was slightly greener in the summer. This part of Nayarit sat at the base of the low range of mountains, and they stood, stark against the sky in the distance, but Preston wasn't really interested in the view.

It wasn't home; that's all that mattered.

Also, there were the giant conundrums running all over the acreage that he would never understand.

Horses. Why anybody would want to keep *horses*.

"Let me run Preacher some," he said, "then tell me where we need to put the supplies."

The scorched grasses of the pastureland were rough on Preacher's feet, so he stuck to the dirt road, but it was late in the day in the summer, so they didn't run long. When he got back to the tower, he found Damien and Buddy at a desk in the corner. At the main desk, a guy in a sweat-soaked T-shirt worked the microphone in Spanish while he kept his eyes on the old-school electronic air maps.

"I know it doesn't look like it," Buddy was saying, mopping his brow with a battered bandana, "but it's rush hour up there. Every recreational pilot at El Chapala wants an excuse to bring supplies and be a hero, but none of them have the balls to land in a field that doesn't have a full concrete runway." Buddy was probably in his fifties, but his hair was a salt-and-pepper froth peeping out from under his wide-brimmed fisherman hat, and his skin was tanned so leathery it was hard to tell if he was originally fair skinned or bronze. It didn't matter—his opinions of the rich ex-pats who gathered by Lake Chapala was obviously not elevated.

"Well, we actually *have* supplies," Damien replied. "Glen told us to bring them, but he didn't tell us where. Do you have *any* idea where he was going?"

Buddy took off his hat and scratched the bald crown of his head, his smile showing a couple of missing teeth and some goodwill. "Well, I don't know where *Glen* thought he was going, but that kid he was chasing down was planning to go here."

He stabbed a stubby finger at a spot on the map so small Damien had to move a big polished glass magnifier over it. "Agujero en la Roca," he read, frowning. "Hole in the Rock? Is that even a town?"

Buddy grimaced. "Well, yes and no. I mean, there's people there, and a church, and one of the best bakeries in Nayarit *or* Jalisco, but I'm not sure if you'd call it a town."

"God, it's overland up the mountains. I don't even think the road goes that way. Do you think I could take the chopper?"

Buddy shook his head. "You could, but you'd need help spotting a place to land it. Frankly, once you hit the tree line, you could fly over a couple of places like la Roca and miss them. You can come up the other side of the mountains, but you'd have to go through Guadalajara, and they're a wasp nest right now, with rescue workers and earthquake damage. Besides, all the emergency vehicles are in Guadalajara for that exact reason."

"Well, how did Glen go there?" Damien said, looking at Preston like he was looking for help.

Preston shrugged. He had no idea either.

"Well, Glen took a motorcycle up the mountain trail to head the kid off—you remember he kept that little two-stroke in the garage? But the kid bought a half-dead horse from some asshole in town who thinks you can keep a horse on a quarter acre of property. So I'm not sure how far the kid got, but that was yesterday morning, and I haven't heard from either of them."

"We heard from them this morning," Damien muttered. "Glen said to bring supplies. Dammit, there's got to be a place to land the chopper."

Buddy shrugged. "I wouldn't count on it. Is the thing prepped for evac?"

Damien rolled his eyes. "Does it *look* like the Black Hawk?"

Preston knew that an air-to-ground evacuation was a tricky business that included carabiners and equipment belts and lifts. He'd seen Damien fly a helicopter while Glen lowered a basket so they could strap a found hiker into the basket and fly him to safety. But an injured person needed care, and setting the basket down gently required people on the other end to guide it down and usually on top of a gurney. There was very little at this tiny airfield that indicated Damien could just fly the chopper two hundred miles and lower a rope.

"We can't go two hundred miles through the mountains on horseback," Damien muttered. "That would take three days minimum—longer if we didn't want to beat the hell out of the horses. And we'd need three horses at least to carry the gear."

"Naw, one extra horse. I've got an all-terrain travois, built it myself. And we can trailer the horses the first two-thirds of the way up the trail. If nothing else, we might pass your brother and that kid out on the road."

"What in the fuck was that kid doing, anyway?" Damien muttered.

"Well, he seemed pretty upset about the town. I gathered he knew somebody there, and there'd been some damage, but there was a lot of him and Glen shouting at each other, and then Glen woke up yesterday morning and the kid had taken off."

Damien's eyes popped open. "I'm assuming Glen packed bungee cord, rope, and handcuffs for when they caught up with each other." Their client was paying a *lot* to make sure Cash Harper got home.

"I'm pretty sure he was packing a tranq gun, truth to tell," Buddy said, cackling. "I tell you what, I have never *seen* Glen Echo so stirred up. That kid's giving him hell or I can't read signs." He smiled genially at Preston and added, "And I can read signs."

Preston smiled back, thinking Damien must have told Buddy what they'd been talking about on the flight out. "I'm being perfectly reasonable." He was certain of it.

"I'm sure you are, boy. And it's about goddamned time."

"You're both insane," Damien muttered. "So will we be ready to move in an hour?"

Buddy shook his head. "Did you or did you not see that storm front following you in?"

Damien swore. "It looked like a doozy too."

"Our Doppler says it's clearing out tomorrow morning. Give it an hour, to make sure the flooding in the road's gone down and any mudslides have had their say. I'll have the horse trailer ready around eightish."

"You got a cot in the hangar?" Damien asked, looking at Preston unhappily.

"No." Buddy rolled his eyes. "There's a perfectly good hotel not five miles down the road. I'll take you once I get Miguel situated. He needs a good hour break to let his brain stop buzzing with all that chatter. You fellas unload the supplies into the hangar and gather your stuff. Meet me at the truck after Miguel's break and you can rest up. Tomorrow's gonna be a doozy of a day."

"Horses," Preston said, his disappointment in life's workings acute. "It's really gotta be horses?"

"Sorry, man," Damien said sincerely. "But don't worry. I know one end from another."

Buddy snickered. "You should. You act like the ass end often enough."

Damien scowled at him. "How long have you been married? Because you can't be paying her enough to stick with that shit."

Buddy chortled. "You think you're so smart. Wait until I bring you dinner. Martha adores you, but she doesn't let anyone talk shit about me."

"I have no idea why."

Buddy just laughed some more and sent Damien and Preston to take care of the plane.

Secret Nights

MARTHA came by right after they'd finished unloading and refueling the Cessna, and Damien embraced her happily. As beautiful as her husband was homely, Martha was still comfortably middle-aged, with enough softness on her body to make hugging her a joy.

Damien's words about his parents had been the truest things he'd said in a while—his mother was all sharp angles and cheekbones, and his father was hard muscle with zero compromise. Hugging women like Martha and Belinda gave him back something from his childhood that he apparently had missed.

She brought with her a plate of beans, rice, and corn tortillas—simple but filling and tasty—and Preston and Damien were grateful beyond words.

"So awesome not having to find a place to eat," Damien said, wiping his mouth as they ate standing up. "Thank you."

"Well, you're going to need your rest," Martha said in slightly accented English. Damien spoke English, Spanish, French, some Farsi, and some Japanese, but it always took him a little while of listening to people speak before he adapted to the regional differences in a language versus the perfect schoolroom intonations. Talking to Martha tonight would help him talk to perfect strangers in their native tongue in the morning.

"How bad is the damage, have you heard?" Damien knew that if they were taking Buddy's horses, they would be strong and sure-footed Arabian crosses. Buddy bred for endurance and temperament—they might not be the most beautiful creatures in the world, but they would get a rider where he needed to go.

"Reports of rock slides almost all the way across the mountains," Martha told him. "The mountains aren't that high up, but it still makes for difficult going. And with the storm washing in tonight, it's going to be even more dangerous—the mountains are soft here, and flash floods happen. It might take you more than just tomorrow. I see bedrolls there. Did you bring a tent too?"

Damien shook his head. "No room, not if we're bringing supplies to the village—and for us. I've been caught out with no supplies before. Don't want to do *that* again."

He'd meant for Martha to laugh, but she only looked concerned. "That was rough," she said softly. "Glen told us how close a thing it was—how very lucky you and your friends were."

"Luck only got us so far," Damien said frankly. "If Tevyn and Mallory hadn't been resourceful, I would have died up there. They spent an entire day boiling snow so they could keep a poultice going. I would have gone into sepsis without it."

Preston gasped, and Damien glanced at him, surprised to see his eyes as big as saucers.

"You didn't tell me that," Preston said. "You talk a lot about them saving your life, but you never tell me *how*."

Damien shrugged. "Well, besides building a fire and keeping the wound clean and me hydrated, they also took me with them when they decided to go down the mountain. I mean they dragged me across the snow until we decided to try that airplane wing as a sled."

"They're very good friends," Martha said soothingly. She looked at Preston. "Did you doubt it?"

Preston shook his head, his eyes staying low, and Damien wondered what he was thinking.

Martha winked at Damien and took his napkin from him, then collected Preston's. "You two are done?"

"Yes, Martha," Preston said, eyes still downcast. "Thank you."

"I think Buddy is going to take you to the hotel. Preston, can you and Preacher ride in the truck bed?"

Preston's head came up, and he flashed a relieved smile at her. "Oh, yes. As long as you don't go too fast, Preacher will be so happy not to get inside a vehicle again today." Preston didn't do great in the heat—his body wasn't great at self-regulation, and since Buddy's truck didn't have air-conditioning, it would be cooler in the back. Damien also knew that the whooshing of the air in the back of the truck actually calmed him down if he got overstimulated.

Martha laughed delightedly and left, taking what was left of the meal to Buddy and telling them to grab their duffel and get into the truck while she went.

"What was that look?" Damien asked. "When I was talking about being on the mountain."

"You don't give me any details," Preston muttered. "You keep telling me they saved your life, but you don't tell me how they *actually* saved your life. I didn't know Tevyn almost died getting the first aid kit until today. I certainly didn't know they cooked your leg until the fever broke."

Damien shrugged. "I wasn't really conscious for a lot of that," he admitted. "I was sort of in and out. But the doctors said it saved my life. But why does it matter? I don't get the grudge you've been carrying against Mal and Tevyn anyway. They didn't desert me—they left me with you and your brother."

"I wanted to be the one to save you," Preston said, his scowl suggesting this was something he hadn't wanted to admit. "And I couldn't. I don't have much to give you, but saving you, that would have been something."

Damien frowned, trying to follow his logic. "But Preston, you weren't going to be up on that mountain. We can't be there all the time for each other. You spend entire weeks away on training missions with your dogs. Sometimes you just have to let the other person out of your sight and hope!"

"But you... you smile for them. For both of them. Since the crash, they're the *only* ones you smile for!"

Oh. Damien grimaced. "Mallory's still afraid to fly," he said, searching in his head for words. "It just... I felt like less of a loser. I had less to live up to, I guess. You and your brother, you... you expect me to be brave."

"You're always brave," Preston said staunchly.

"Not with you." It was a hard admission to make, and he wasn't sure what he expected. Preston opened his mouth and then shut it again, and just when Damien thought the conversation was over, Preston finally found words.

"God, I wish it could have been me up there."

"I'm so glad it wasn't." Damien closed his eyes. "If the infection hadn't killed me, worrying about you would have. Besides, you were down on the bottom of the mountain looking for us, and you will *never* know how much that meant to me, to hear your voice when I was still strapped to the back of that sled."

"I was so worried," Preston said, holding out his hand and whistling for Preacher to jump into the pickup bed. Preacher actually backed up to get a running jump, and then sailed over the side of the pickup, no tailgate necessary. "Good boy, Preacher. Such a good boy. So smart." Preston clicked his tongue, which was apparently Preacher's notice that he could lick Preston's face. One, two, three licks, and then Preston clicked again and Preacher went back to nuzzling. Damien was always so impressed—Preston and his dogs could practically read each other's minds.

"I didn't mean to make you worry." Damien's voice dropped, and for a moment he was mesmerized. Preston's angelic face, for once relaxed and at peace, captured him. No scowling, no hyper-focused glare, no eyes in the distance. Just Preston, open and happy and soft.

Preston glanced at him and tilted his head. "What? What is that look?"

Damien swallowed against a sudden dryness in his throat. "I don't know what you're talking about," he rasped.

A slow smile bloomed over Preston's face—one that had more "fallen" than "angel" in it.

"I know what you're thinking," he said smugly.

"*I* don't even know what I'm thinking." Preston's hands were big and capable, and for a moment Damien was focused on *them* and the way Preston liked to be touched firmly, without teasing, and how he'd probably touch Damien just like that.

Everywhere. Preston would touch him *everywhere*.

For once, Preston met his eyes. "I want you in my mouth," he said. "Some people don't like the taste of come, but I do."

Damien almost choked on his tongue, and then all he could do was gape, mouth opening and closing, a terrified and confused fish.

Preston's chuckle, low and evil, skittered up his spine. "And now I know what you're thinking for *sure*," he said before turning away. Damien wasn't sure if Preston was letting him get his composure or just didn't have anything else to say.

Either way he was right—heated images of what the two of them would be like together were now filtering through Damien's brain, and he had to remind himself repeatedly that just because Preston said he wanted it to happen didn't mean that it would.

"I'll sit in the back with the dog," Preston said cheerfully as Buddy rounded the corner. Damien nodded and hopped into the front of the battered vehicle, relieved when Buddy gave his wife one last lingering kiss and hopped in to drive.

"You look terrified. Did you hear from Glen again?" Buddy said bluntly as he pulled off onto the dusty blacktop and started heading toward town in the setting of a brutal sun. They passed Buddy's pastureland, where twenty to thirty horses ran in a welcome breeze, separated into pens of three or so. Pretty animals, some of them recently brushed and gleaming, some of them dusty and proud of it. Damien remembered that he'd be riding tomorrow, and a part of him cheered up. He was *good* with horses, and boy wouldn't it be fun to be back in *that* saddle again.

"No," Damien muttered. "Because that would mean his cell phone wasn't dying and he wasn't flying by the seat of his pants."

Buddy laughed shortly but then looked back to Damien. "So if it's not Glen, what's got you so puckered? Life's too short to eat lemons, boy."

Without meaning to, Damien glanced back behind them, to the back of Preston's head as he sat easily in the pickup, Preacher on his lap. He probably loved it back there—nothing but the wind in his ears, no human interaction to bother him.

But Buddy caught the look. "He's been waiting for you a long time," he said.

"And he wants me *now*?" Damien asked bitterly.

"What's wrong with you now?"

"God, it's just like talking to Preston," he muttered. "Except *you* don't want to sleep with me!"

"No, I do not," Buddy laughed. "But I do want to see you boys happy. How long have I known you?"

What was it, ten years ago? Before they'd exited the service, when Glen had first bought the AS350. They'd been on leave and had wanted to take a recreational flight, and Preston had wanted to come with them. Some place the dogs could run, he'd said. Buddy's airstrip had been on a list of possible landings in Mexico, and boy, Glen had liked the idea of flying out of the country and hiking someplace not Napa. Preston had brought Coop, Preacher's daddy, and they'd spent two weeks in this little-known part of Mexico, and then a week in a tiny coast town up from Puerto Vallarta. Buddy had been their friend and their fishing buddy and their guide, and when his horses had broken loose from one of his pastures, the three of them had jumped at the chance to help.

Glen had flown up and spotted the horses, and Damien had lowered himself from the chopper on a line and coaxed Buddy's best mare to a halter and saddle blanket. He'd ridden her back, and the others had followed, and Buddy had been their biggest fan ever since.

The experience had given them the idea for their rescue service, actually, and Buddy had been one of their best contacts when they'd started it up.

Of course the flip side was that he felt compelled to comment on their lives—and that he knew Glen, Damien, and Preston really damned well.

"Too long," Damien said now in response to his question.

"Long enough," Buddy corrected. "He had the biggest crush on you ten years ago. It's not a crush anymore."

Damien swallowed. "What would you call it now?" he asked, grateful for the wind coming in from their open windows. This conversation would sound unbearably serious if they weren't shouting over the roar of air in their ears.

"Same thing you feel for him, of course," Buddy said. "Don't ask me to spell it out for you, Damien. You're supposedly grown."

"He's Glen's little brother," Damien said unnecessarily. "If I fuck this up, I fuck up my whole life."

Buddy snorted. "Well, if it was anybody else but Glen Echo, that might be the case, but Glen would probably be just fine calling the two of you morons and riding you for screwing up a perfectly good friendship for the rest of your lives. Wouldn't ditch you as a friend. He just wouldn't let you forget you somehow managed to fuck up the best relationship you've ever had."

"How would you even know that!" Damien asked, laughing. "For all you know, I've got a choice of hot young celebrity chefs and fashion designers just dying to make me their action adventure boy toy!"

"How would I know?" Buddy risked a look at him while keeping both hands on the wheel for the uncertain road. "Boy, that's the first time since you came down off that mountain that you even tried to entertain me with your foolishness. Now tell me, did you do that healing in your heart all by yourself, or was it getting stuck in the cockpit while that kid worried out the splinter in your heart?"

Damien let out a little bark of laughter. "So that's a no on the celebrity chef/fashion designer prospect?" he asked just to make sure, but this time Buddy didn't smile.

"What's the worst that can happen, Damie? You sleep with your best friend's little brother and you two complete each other and you don't have to ever be alone in your hearts again?"

"That's not awful!" Damien retorted.

"Well, then, why don't you shoot for that and see what happens!" Buddy told him. "Now, which hotel do you want? The one with the fountains in the middle and the veranda and the four-star restaurant in the quad, or the one that says, 'I'm getting up at the crack of dawn to trailer horses and then ride them all over Mexico'?"

"Well, if your wife hadn't just fed us, I'd take the four-star restaurant," Damien said, disgruntled. "Does the crack-of-dawn one at least have a breakfast place nearby?"

"It does indeed. There's a diner around the corner. I'll pick you two up there around eight thirty, and if you're late, you'll have to wait for me to eat my chorizo and eggs, because they're delicious."

"Will you make us wait for that even if we're early?" Damien asked, because sometimes that extra ten minutes of sleep could make the difference between a good day and a bad one.

"Probably."

"Eight thirty-five it will be."

"Then this is your hotel." Buddy pulled up to a small set of cottages, worn but repaired, with freshly painted yellow trim. "I'll wait for you to check in, and if you don't tell 'em about the dog, they won't mind about the dog, if you take my meaning."

Damien did. Especially with one of Preston's dogs. Preacher was too well-behaved to be a nuisance, and his brindle coat was more guard hair than undercoat, so there was a minimum of shedding.

"I do." He swung out and went to the main cabin, asking for a room with two queens, which they didn't have.

Of course they didn't have a room with two queens.

"A single king-sized?" he asked, not wanting to make a big deal out of this because he'd slept in lots of beds with lots of guys with no sex involved. A mattress and clean sheets was a mattress and clean sheets—sex only had to happen if the two people involved wanted to see each other naked.

You really want to see him naked.

He wants to taste your come.

Damien shuddered. It was raw and crude, but that's not how Preston had meant it. He'd been blunt and honest—and making absolutely certain that Damien knew the consent was all in Damien's court.

"Señor?" The middle-aged woman at the desk smiled warmly at him, and he shrugged.

"We'll take what you've got, darlin'."

"Good. There's a bacon-and-eggs place around the corner," she told him kindly. "And we've got vending machines if you need something, and toiletries if you've forgotten your own."

"Thank you, ma'am. I think we'll be okay."

He rented the room—the room with the one bed—and went outside to give Preston the key and grab his duffel.

Buddy drove off, and Damien and Preston entered the little room.

"It's bigger than most hotels'," Preston observed. The bed dominated the room of course, but there was a small table and a coffee maker in the corner. The walls were stained wood and so was the floor, but a big worn area rug in tan and rose made the place welcoming. Paintings by local artists were on the walls, and Damien had a moment to think this was better than the flop he'd been planning on.

"We usually stay at a crappier place when we're here," he said. "I wonder why Buddy didn't take us there."

"Because he wanted it to be nice," Preston decided, and Damien wouldn't contradict him.

"Maybe." Damien threw his duffel on the bed. "I'm going to hop in the shower and then study our route. Has Preacher peed lately?"

"I'll take him out for a loop around the cabin," Preston said. "I can shower when I get back."

Fair enough.

Damien brought his sleep shorts and T-shirt into the bathroom with him so Preston wouldn't accidentally catch him out naked. He was resigned to Preston seeing the leg by now—even the hardworking AC couldn't counteract the humidity, and the shorts would be more comfortable. Who knew? Maybe the scarring would scare Preston off for good and Damien wouldn't have to answer the hard question, right? When he emerged from the shower after brushing his teeth, he dressed and set the computer up on the table, then activated Glen's satellite tracker and tried to figure out where he was.

Preston came in and laid out a towel for Preacher to lie down on, then disappeared into the shower himself.

When he came out, Damien was deeply engrossed in what the spotty internet had to tell him.

"What are you looking at?" Preston asked, startling Damien because he was standing right behind his chair.

"Oh my God—scared me!" Damien turned his head and then swallowed. Preston was wearing sleep shorts and no shirt. My, his bare chest was really… damn.

Instead of backing up, Preston's hands came down on his shoulders firmly, and he started a warm massage that seemed to loosen up Damien's back muscles whether he was ready for that or not.

"Are you scared now?" Preston asked courteously, digging his thumb into a stubborn muscle at the base of Damien's skull.

Damien gave up and melted, helpless and at his mercy. "No," he mumbled. "I'm interested in where Glen and this Cash kid went, but I'm not scared."

Preston looked over his shoulder, his face close enough that Damien could feel his breaths. "Where do you think they went?"

"See this spot here on the satellite?" Damien said, pointing a vague finger.

"Yes, it looks pretty. Lots of gardens."

"Yeah, but there's no name for it on the map. As far as the map is concerned, the closest thing there is a town that consists of a block of merchants and a block of houses—population maybe three hundred, and most of those are outlying properties."

Preston grunted. "So what's that big house with the columns and the garden doing there?"

"That is a very good question. Oh God, Preston, you are sending me right to sleep."

Because Preston's fingers hadn't stopped moving, and Damien was coming undone.

"Well, go lie on the bed and I can do your leg."

Damien opened his mouth to say no, but Preston rubbed his lips against Damien's cheek and shut down all of Damien's words.

"Now, I know you're going to try to say I don't need to do this," Preston told him. "But I want to. And don't you want me to make your leg better?"

"Where did you learn massage?" Damien asked helplessly.

"I took, like, six anatomy classes, and besides muscle groups, do you know what I learned?" He punctuated this with a solid stroke behind Damien's ear that sent a humming through his groin.

"I have no idea," Damien breathed.

"I learned that touch is good." Preston smoothed his palm along the back of Damien's neck. "Touch makes everything feel better. It strengthens the bonds between all animals—human and otherwise. Touch is good for both of us. Now move."

Damien closed his eyes, about all of his resistance to this moment washed away by Preston's persistence.

He limped to the bed and sat up on it, pillows behind his back, leg extended. Preston went into the bathroom and came out with some all-purpose massage oil and a towel and pulled a chair up next to the bed. He reached out to lift Damien's leg and Damien tensed, because he'd done this exercise a thousand times and didn't need help.

Preston gave him an inscrutable look and laid the towel out underneath it, then rubbed some oil between his palms to get it warm.

He leaned forward to smooth the oil over Damien's skin, and Damien looked away.

"Do you think I'm going to hurt you?" Preston asked, sounding hurt himself as his hands made firm contact with Damien's sensitive skin.

"No," Damien muttered. "I just don't like looking at it."

Preston's hands grew more insistent, and he smoothed the oil over Damien's shin and under his calf, and then again, and again. Damien was conscious of every ridge, divot, and furrow under the skin, into the muscle and bone, that showed how much his leg had lost.

"It's different," Preston said, the heels of his hands going to work in earnest on the cramped flesh behind Damien's knee and his calf. "But not awful. It functions, right?"

Ah! His hands were so warm, so sure. "Barely," Damien said bleakly. "I'm up to three miles." He and Glen used to do ten miles together effortlessly, but Damien had made Glen run on his own because he was so much slower now.

Preston worked higher, up past the kneecap, to where the infection had crawled up to his femur. Damien pulled in a breath, because it hurt, and Preston eased the pressure somewhat.

"This one scared you," he said, running a fearless finger down the inside of Damien's knee.

"If the operation hadn't worked, they would have had to amputate," Damien said. He shuddered. "It was touch and go."

To his surprise, Preston bent and kissed the outside of the leg. "I would have missed the leg," he said. "But I would have still kissed whatever spot was there for me to kiss."

Damien swallowed. Preston was there, so close—his expression intent, his hands sending warm, drugging pulses down Damien's leg. His muscles were relaxing, melting, and tension drained from him in waves.

He wasn't sure he was going to do it until he actually saw his own hand, reaching out to cup Preston's cheek. Preston stayed intent on what he was doing, but he smiled a little and leaned into the touch.

"Nice," he said. "Now lean back. I'm going to touch you some more. Do I have your consent?"

Damien's eyes flew open, and he dropped his hand. "Uhm—"

Preston met his eyes, and Damien's heart slowed to a crawl, every beat loud in his ears. "I promise, Damie, I won't let anything bad happen to us. Don't you trust me?"

"How are you going to touch me?" Damien asked through a dry throat. "Clinically, like this or—"

"Intimately," Preston told him, no embarrassment whatsoever. "Please?" He bit his lip in an uncharacteristic show of uncertainty. "You look so beautiful."

All the oxygen in the entire world disappeared. Damien couldn't draw a breath. He bit his lip too, suddenly shy in front of this person he'd known for years.

"O... okay." He couldn't believe it was his own voice.

Preston wiped his hands on the towel he'd brought and rose up off the chair enough to hover directly over Damien. "I'll start with a kiss."

Now Damien was the one who couldn't meet his eyes. He closed them instead and lifted his face, not sure what to expect.

Firm lips moving on his came first, and then Preston's shaky exhale against his face. Damien gasped, parting his mouth, and Preston made sort of a humming sound, followed by his tongue as he took charge of the kiss in the same way he'd taken charge of Damien's leg, of the conversation in the plane, of their relationship change from the start.

Confidently, with absolute focus.

Damien hummed back, opening his arms and taking Preston's weight on top of him as they explored. Preston's skin slid, smooth and taut, under Damien's palms, and Preston wasn't shy about leaning into Damien's touch or humming with appreciation.

The encouragement worked, the happy sounds, the way Preston undulated against him, and Damien found his own responses growing urgent. Preston moved his hand under Damien's shirt, exploring his abdomen, his chest, his—*oh my God!*

"Your nipples are *very* sensitive," Preston said with satisfaction, pinching one and then the other while Damien wriggled his hips against the bed in an attempt to stay still.

"You think?" Damien gasped.

"I just said so. What will happen if I suck on one?" Preston was regarding him with curiosity and deep joy.

"I have no idea," Damien muttered, arching off the bed again. On one level, he was being facetious, but on the most basic level he was telling the absolute truth. As far as he knew, Preston's mouth against his sensitive skin might send him catapulting off the bed— or worse—it might send his cock into orgasm overload and he'd climax right there.

"Let's see." Preston's knees were on the side of the bed next to Damien's hips, and he rucked up Damien's shirt and bent his head, licking experimentally.

Damien gasped and tried not to whimper. *Oh hell oh damn oh....* "I'm gonna come if you don't stop!"

Preston pulled back and gazed at him, a look of utter enchantment on his face. "Really? Wow! That's *incredible*. Are you always this sensitive?"

Damien fell back against the pillows, panting, completely out of fight and out of pride. "I have no idea. I haven't had sex in almost two years. For all I know, the doctors rewired my whole body and my nipples are like teeny-tiny little penises." He felt like his sex drive was exploding out of his skin.

Preston smoothed a hand back through his hair, gentling him almost like he would one of the dogs.

"I understand," he said softly. "This is new all over again, and special."

Damien's eyes began to sting. "Preston, did you think it wouldn't be special with you?"

"Because we care about each other," Preston said, licking at Damien's nipple again—but softly this time.

"Yes," Damien admitted, trying hard to knot his fingers in Preston's short hair. "Suck on it? Please? I'm… I'm going to come too soon, but I'm dying here and—"

"And we're going to do this more than once," Preston told him, and that eye contact, from Preston, was more intimate than his mouth on Damien's flesh. "Because we care about each other."

"Yes," Damien said, conceding in a rush. His body sagged against the bed, still throbbing from arousal, but all of the fight was gone, all the self-restraint. There was nothing left other than his desire to give in to Preston's desires, to Preston's skillful, no-bullshit lovemaking, and to enjoy whatever Preston wanted to do with him.

It had been so long since he'd felt good about himself—about *anything*.

"Good," Preston almost purred. He bent his head again, playing with Damien's nipples, raising his arousal to a fever pitch, and just when Damien was about to lose his mind, right before he started begging so loud every resident of Las Varas would come running to make sure he wasn't being eaten by a dragon, Preston raised his head and said, "I'm going to touch your cock now. I'll push your underwear down so it won't get messy."

Damien might have gasped, "Sure, okay, go ahead," but he was never sure how. He thought the air on his overheated skin was like another touch, and then Preston's big callused hand wrapped around him and that thought was a lie.

"Oh God," he gasped. "Preston, I'm gonna—oh God—"

Preston pulled his head back. "I can suck your cock or I can kiss you and keep you quiet," he said, completely sober. "Which one do you want?"

And usually Damien would have picked the blowjob, because who *wouldn't* pick the blowjob, but Preston's clean smell of sunshine and exercise and dogs was permeating Damien's senses, and they'd only now started kissing, and he found he hungered for it, wanted that contact even more than the sexual release his body was screaming for.

"Kiss me," he begged, and Preston's mouth on his, invading, taking ownership, was a heaven he would never have guessed.

And true to his word, Preston's hand kept up that mesmerizing stroke, long, hard, without mercy, until Damien's begging whimpers were muffled by Preston's insatiable kiss.

"Please!" he pleaded, not even sure what he was pleading for, but Preston seemed to know.

He pulled back and gave Damien a pillow. "When we're at my house, in the cabin in the back, you can make as much noise as you want," he promised, and then he lowered his head to Damien's cock and Damien screamed into the pillow.

Ah! So good! His body was so sensitized, so needy, it didn't take much—a stroke of Preston's hand, a swirl of his tongue, the delicious pressure of his mouth, sucking hard—

He screamed again, body arching from the bed, come boiling from his balls, his entire body exploding in white light and sweet, sweet release.

Preston kept milking him with his mouth, and aftershocks rocked Damien's body for a couple of minutes until he pushed lightly on Preston's shoulder in discomfort.

"Tender," he murmured, and Preston popped off and swallowed messily.

"Scoot over," he commanded, and Damien scooched his body sideways so they could both lie on the bed, facing each other. Damien reached up with a thumb and wiped some of the glaze from Preston's lips and chin, and Preston grinned at him without shame.

"Good?"

"I'm very relaxed now," Damien said primly, and Preston's grin went wider.

"That's good."

"Would you like me to, uhm…." Damien reached down between them and stroked him through his shorts.

Preston arched happily against the pressure of his hand. "If you want to," he purred, and Damien shook hard with how very much he wanted to.

"Yes," he whispered. But first he had to kiss Preston again, taste the sunshine of his grin, taste his own earthiness on Preston's lips.

Preston returned the kiss with interest, and Damien's slow stroke turned urgent as Preston thrust up against him.

"Slow down," he panted, pulling back a little. "Here, help me—"

Preston lifted his hips and helped strip himself of the shorts and briefs underneath.

Damien got a look and swallowed. "Nice," he muttered, because Preston's flesh had felt huge in his palm, but it looked even bigger thrusting palely under the dim overhead light.

"Do you want to know how many inches it is?" Preston asked wickedly.

Damien rolled his eyes. "No. I *never* want to know how many inches it is. Not length, not girth, not distance from your balls."

Preston laughed and leaned in and whispered three outrageous numbers into Damien's ear that somehow made what they were doing raw and real.

"It's a good thing I top," Damien gasped, and Preston's laugh grew filthier.

"Not anymore."

Damien opened his mouth to argue, but Preston kissed him, and Damien's hand found his cock all over again.

He shivered, because holding a man was a sensual pleasure all its own, and he broke off the kiss to explore Preston's body.

It didn't get any worse without clothes.

Preston was stringy and fit, all of it from being happily active with his dogs. He wasn't grotesquely defined, but his muscles were everywhere, including his chest, and as Damien kissed down it, Preston said, "I like my nipples played with too," with so much hope in his voice Damien had to chuckle.

And then he had to taste, just to see how true it was.

Preston made that very singular humming noise again, and Damien sucked hard, laving the end with his tongue to make up for the sharpness.

"Ouch," Preston murmured. "Good ouch. More!"

Oh, this was fun. Preston's body wasn't fragile, and he wasn't ticklish. He liked firm touches, and lots of them. Damien glutted his palms on smooth golden skin and the muscle underneath, and Preston encouraged him with every touch.

By the time Damien got down to Preston's rather splendid erection, he was aroused again, and dying to taste.

Ah! It was every bit as firm and as satisfying in his mouth as it had been in his palm, but with the added sweet and salty taste of the slick fluid at the end.

Preston spread his legs and rocked his hips rhythmically while Damien sucked, the in-and-out motion unmistakable. Damien stroked the base with his fist and swirled his tongue around the head while Preston hummed his encouragement, and Damien found he was arching his hips against the bed, his own cock erect and aroused again.

"Swing your—oh, that's nice. Swing your bottom this way," Preston murmured. "I'm going to touch your asshole—is that okay?"

Damien almost stopped what he was doing, because he hadn't lied to Preston—he'd been the giver since he'd first started having sex. But Preston slid his palm down Damien's backside, the same firm, all-encompassing touch he seemed to like himself, and Damien shuddered.

He found that he'd repositioned himself on the bed without consciously saying yes, and as Preston's finger, slick with lubricant that he'd apparently hidden behind the pillow, touched Damien's cleft, he groaned around Preston's cock, aware that he just might have to stop this blowjob if things got any more intense.

Preston's finger slid in to the first knuckle and wiggled around, and Damien opened his mouth, thinking he was going to give a polite "no, thank you," but instead he dropped his head to Preston's thigh and groaned again.

And reached back behind him with one hand and spread his cheeks, because God, he wanted more.

"Oh, good," Preston said happily. "That's a yes, right?"

He slid the finger in deeper, and Damien found himself in a totally undignified position chanting, "Yes, yes, yes, yes…."

Preston added another finger, and Damien went sprawling across his legs, facedown, embarrassed and aroused beyond endurance.

"Wait," he moaned. "Can I just… you know… get up or—"

Preston pulled out both fingers, and Damien found himself manhandled, for once outweighed and out-muscled by his partner.

"I'd put you on your hands and knees," Preston said practically, positioning Damien on his back, "but that would hurt your leg to bend like that. Here—I'm going to bend this leg right… like… this—" And he put it over his shoulder. "—and stretch this other leg and…." Preston bent Damien's weak leg gently at the knee and set his foot on the bed, then, oh wow, put his fingers back into play.

Damien's mind went blank with dark, exquisite pleasure, and he closed his eyes. Conveniently, he forgot that he hadn't done it this way since high school and that hadn't ended well, and that he liked to take charge. He forgot that he was vulnerable, at Preston's mercy, and he'd always imagined being the one leading during this moment, and he forgot that he'd been trying not to imagine this moment at all. He even forgot his dignity.

All his traitorous body remembered—*all* it remembered—was that he trusted Preston, and Preston would never hurt him.

Preston pulled out his fingers and replaced them with his cock, and thrust carefully inside.

Damien's eyes flew open as his body was invaded, and he shook, sweat breaking out across his shoulders and throat.

It hurt, but it didn't, and it was full, too full, but it was wonderful, and it needed to stop, but he didn't want it to end. He closed his eyes and tried to relax, allowing the inevitable to happen.

And still Preston thrust, until his head popped in, and Damien took a breath, trembling.

"Good?" Preston asked, kissing his forehead, his cheeks, his closed eyes. "Is this good?"

"It's amazing," Damien said on a shaky breath. It had been so long since he'd been new to sex, he'd almost forgotten what it felt like at all. "Don't stop."

"Oh, thank God." Preston thrust all the way in, until Damien didn't think he could take any more, and then he pulled gently out. Damien gasped, clenching because he didn't want the sensation to end, and then Preston pressed forward again, and now he cried out in bliss.

The timeless rhythm continued, and Damien's sounds grew guttural, animal, as his body pitched higher and higher. Preston's hums became grunts, and Damien opened his eyes to see Preston's back bowed, his neck straining as he fucked Damien senseless into the mattress.

Damien remembered how to be an active participant then, not a receptacle, coming undone. He lifted his fingers to Preston's nipples and pinched, and ran his hands over Preston's neck and shoulders and biceps. Preston hummed again, and his thrusts went triple time, until Damien's vision washed black and then white, every synapse in his body exploding into light.

His orgasm shook him, from the soles of his feet to his chest to his core, leaving him helpless and liquid. As he melted into the bed, his clenching muscles relaxing, Preston moaned and slowed his next thrust with careful control, hitting himself right… right… just….

Preston groaned, shuddering, spending into Damien's body in long, slow pulses, and Damien realized he hadn't asked Preston's health status before they'd come together.

His own was clear—had been when he'd been in the crash, had been the months prior, and he hadn't done anything to change it since.

As Preston fell on top of him, he realized how undone he'd been, how much he'd needed this, Preston's touch, Preston's sex, all of it—if he'd been so lost he hadn't even asked, he'd been made of need.

"No condoms," he muttered, confused and a little afraid.

"Status clear," Preston said into his ear. "I use condoms with everybody but you, tested after my last partner."

Damien moaned a little, his body still shaking in the throes of orgasm. "Can't believe I didn't—"

"You knew I'd take care of you," Preston said with an unconscious arrogance that probably should have pissed Damien off.

But as he lay there, under Preston's heavy body, marked thoroughly by his sex and his spend, he realized that all he had in him was relief.

Preston was going to take care of him. Oh God—somebody would.

DAMIEN'S phone went off at seven thirty in the morning, and he groaned and fought his way from the tangle of Preston's limbs so he could stop it. Preston wrapped arms and legs around him again and retangled the both of them, his every move eloquent of possession.

"Preston," Damien mumbled. "We need to get up."

"No."

Damien struggled to sit upright. "What do you mean no?"

Preston sat up and scowled at him. "I liked last night better!"

"Go figure," Damien rasped, getting a grumpy smile from Preston and returning it.

Well, who wouldn't like last night better? Damien had fallen asleep, tired and used and—holy wow!—pain-free for the first time in forever. Preston had gathered him in, possessive and careful and with a minimum of conversation, which Damien appreciated because his head was racing enough for the both of them.

He wasn't sure when he'd been awakened, Preston's hands stroking his flanks, his abdomen, his chest.

"I want you again," Preston had whispered, his voice calming the ricocheting thoughts that had haunted Damien even in his dreams.

"Okay," Damien mumbled, because he couldn't find words for why they shouldn't. Were there words for why they shouldn't? There were probably words for why this was a bad thing, but right then, with Preston's hands moving to Damien's hips, positioning him just so, with his cock—and boy, wasn't *that* a surprise—newly slicked and thrusting at Damien's entrance, Damien couldn't imagine what those words would be.

As Preston started to thrust, one hand on Damien's hip, the other arm under Damien's head as they spooned, the chaos in Damien's head gave way to one clear, inarticulate focus—and that was Preston's body and what it was doing to his own.

After Preston gave a hard, bottoming thrust and bit Damien's shoulder, shaking with the force of his climax, Damien gave a smaller shudder, completely depleted and happy. He clutched Preston's hand to his chest for a moment, not wanting to let go.

His body was perfect, liquid and satiated, and whatever his brain had been chewing on, that was so unimportant, Damien couldn't even remember what it was.

Now, with the cold light of morning searing through the curtains, Damien was starting to have a clue.

"You know, Preston," he said carefully after their shared morning grump, "maybe we should—"

Preston kissed him, hard, possessively, uncompromising.

He released Damien's mouth and scowled. "There's no changing last night," he said.

Damien's cock gave a little perk of arousal, and Damien almost looked at it and told it to stand down. "I know that," he muttered bleakly.

"It's morning, and your brain is going to come up with all sorts of things. Words. You and Glen, all those fucking words."

"Words are important, Preston," he said, and Preston's snort told him that lesson was not ever going to be learned.

"Are your words saying we shouldn't do this again?"

Damien opened his mouth to say yes, probably they should make it a one-time thing, and Preston harrumphed again.

"Your words are wrong," he stated. "We should be doing this all the time."

"We have to eat sometimes," Damien said mildly.

"That's a lying thing," Preston said, scowl intensifying. "Where you're trying to be funny but you're distracting me. What are you telling Glen?"

Oh God. "That I slept with his little brother?" Glen could only break his nose once over this, right?

"Are. Sleeping," Preston said, no bullshit in his voice. "I went to school. I know grammar."

Damien opened his mouth once, and then acknowledged the change the verb tense made. "More?"

Preston's head tilt had more than a little bit of presumption in it. "Not now. You just said we had to get up and get ready."

"I meant you want to do this more? Later?"

"I want us to sleep in the same bed a lot, Damien. I want us to have sex a lot. I told you—I want to fix up the cottage in the back so you don't have to put a pillow over your mouth. You can scream every night."

"But I have an apartment in the city," Damien muttered, feeling dumb. He and Glen shared it, as a matter of fact, because some of their clients had personal helicopters and rooftop helipads, and those were the people they tried to serve immediately.

"Glen can serve those clients. We can fix you up a room at the hangar for big jobs. You can live with me."

And a part of Damien leaped for joy. A home? A real home, not just a place to crash, where Glen might be getting lucky in the next room? Or Damien, sometimes, but that life had begun to pall even before the crash. It was why, perhaps, Damien had put so much into his useless crush on Mallory Armstrong. His childhood home had been cold and beautiful—and he'd left it behind for a clean barracks and a brotherhood.

And then he'd left that behind for freedom and his brother.

But a place with a couch and throw pillows, with dogs and warmth—hell, with a baby across the backyard, if Belinda and Ozzy had their way—

"I'm not moving in with you after one good night," Damien said, because his rapidly beating heart was a traitorous traitor who traited.

"No," Preston said, oblivious to Damien's wobbly voice, his complete lostness. "You'll move in with me because we care about each other, and you like having sex with me, and because we would have a good home together." He grinned. "You said it yourself—a home with dogs is a good home."

Something about the word *home* hurt. Damien swallowed and went to roll out of bed before Preston stopped him, a hand on his arm. "This isn't over. I won't forget this conversation. And we are sleeping in the same bag, the same bed, and the same place whenever we're together. Are we clear?"

Damien opened his mouth to say, "No, Preston, you can't just dictate a relationship like that!" But Preston stopped him with two fingers on his lips.

"I'm sorry. That was rude. I *want* us to sleep in the same place whenever we're together. Can we do that?"

Maybe it was the way he said it—like a schoolboy being forced to learn his lessons. Maybe it was the fact that he had tried, with no prompting whatsoever, to not be an autocratic asshole who dictated the terms of the relationship, when Preston had always known exactly what he wanted and obviously had no shame going for it.

And maybe it was the way his fingers felt on Damien's lips.

"This…." Oh God. "This won't be the end," Damien conceded.

Preston's slow smile made him wonder what *Preston* thought he'd said. "That means it's a beginning. Excellent. Do you want to shower?" He sniffed experimentally. "We both smell like sex. This might be the last time we can have warm water for a while."

"Sure," Damien said.

"You go first, and I'll take Preacher out to pee."

Damien looked over to where Preacher was sleeping on his towel, a travel bowl of water and one of food placed neatly by his front paws.

"He's such a good boy," Damien murmured. The dog had gotten up once in the middle of the night, paced around the room steadily, sniffing all the corners, and then had gone directly back to his blanket.

A dog that smart knew when he was being talked about, and his eyebrows went up hopefully.

"All dogs are good boys," Preston said fondly. "But Preacher is the best."

Preacher lifted his head and shoulders, and Preston got out of bed and reached for his sleep shorts and T-shirt—but left the underwear where he'd put them: neatly folded on the bed stand.

"Forgot something," Damien said, looking at the underwear and thinking about Preston just freeballing as he took Preacher for his morning walk.

Preston regarded him, perplexed. "I barely wore them last night," he said. "I'm going to want to wear them after my shower. Why would I put them on now when I smell like sex?" That self-satisfied grin popped out. "Lots of sex."

Damien wasn't going to fault his logic—what would he say? *"Preston, your big swinging dick might frighten onlookers?"*

"Never mind," he said faintly. "I'll be out in five."

In the shower he took stock, thinking that the "pleasant" soreness of his backside might not be so pleasant after three days on horseback, but otherwise nicely surprised.

His leg felt amazingly good after Preston's ministrations. He seemed to remember Preston's bold fingers kneading and relaxing his muscles as he drifted off to sleep the second time, and a part of him was shamed for thinking Preston didn't understand what it was they'd done. Preston understood that touch increased the bond between two people—or a man and his dog—and he knew what he was doing for Damien when he touched him.

As far as Preston was concerned, sex was a way to make their bond deeper, stronger—better.

Are you ready for that?

Damien thought about that little voice in his head as he soaped up again. Was that his problem? Not that Preston might not understand the implications of two friends having sex, but that Damien wasn't ready for them?

What if I hurt him?

Damien found himself swallowing rapidly, his chest tightening, his jaw growing so taut his ears hurt.

Oh.

That was the root of his problem.

Damien didn't know how to live a happy ever after. Preston seemed to—but what if Damien got it wrong? What if Damien ended up hurting the person he cared for the most?

You were Glen's friend first.

Yeah, but Glen couldn't do what Preston just did.

Damien would *die* for Glen Echo—he'd established that in basic training, when their master sergeant had been spit-yelling in Damien's face so hard, Damien felt like his eyeballs were rupturing. Sarge had turned toward another green recruit, and across from him, Glen had been wiping his own face in sympathy. Damien had risked a look at their CO and then had wiped his face in earnest, and as Sarge had turned around, they'd both stared straight ahead, innocent as little soldier angels.

Damien couldn't love another human being the way he loved Glen.

But that thing he and Preston had done in bed the night before… that was very, very different from how Damien felt about his buddy, his brother, his best friend.

As Damien got out of the shower and dried off, then put his underwear back on because Preston was right—they hadn't worn their underwear for long at all—he heard Preston and an ecstatic Preacher coming back inside.

"Good boy," Preston said, his voice echoing into the bathroom. "Such a good boy. Took that big ol' crap behind the cabin where nobody saw. So good. Here, have a treat. Such a good dog!"

Damien imagined Preston, fondling Preacher's ears, stroking his back and his flanks, scratching him at the base of the tail, and his entire body shuddered—including his own well-used ass.

Preston had touched *him* all over too.

Maybe Preston had it right. Touch was a deeper bond, steadfast, closer.

Damien felt like Preston was a part of him now in a way no human being had ever been.

Yeah, Damien would still die for Glen, but the things he'd do for Preston became gigantic, unfathomable, and frightening.

His body tingled, remembering their moments of touch from the night before.

Preston had called last night a beginning. An unexpected thrill of exhilaration shook Damien to the center of his being, a tingling that was at once wholly sexual and wholly emotional too.

For the first time, he wondered what could come next, if a change between two people could *start* with a night like that.

Maybe that's what he was thinking when he left the bathroom wearing a towel instead of his briefs. Maybe he wasn't thinking about anything at all, or maybe he was overthinking something that had simply felt good and he'd like to repeat.

No matter what he was *thinking*, when Preston emerged five minutes later, a towel around his waist, Damien hadn't dressed yet and was, instead, staring at the satellite pictures of that little place called Hole in the Rock.

"Didn't we do this last night?" Preston asked, looking over his shoulder again.

"I swear, it looks like a resort hotel," Damien muttered. "I just can't figure out what would make that kid steal a mangy horse and risk Glen's wrath by escaping to get there."

He became acutely aware of Preston's steamy body behind his, and of the extra forty-five minutes they had to get someplace maybe ten minutes away.

He turned slightly in his chair and put a tentative hand on Preston's flank, thinking that Preston's body was even more beautiful in the sunlight coming in above the curtain valances than he had been in the lamplight the night before.

"What are you doing?" Preston asked, although it sounded like he had a pretty good idea.

Damien closed his eyes and buried his face against Preston's taut stomach. "I'm appreciating your body," he said.

Preston's low chuckle told him he understood better than Damien probably wished. With a quick, focused movement, he ripped off the towel and revealed himself as semihard already.

"Do you appreciate it now?"

Damien lifted his length and stroked it, and then lowered his head, taking it in, heat, length, girth.

Preston made that sound again—it was starting to resonate in Damien's bones—and Damien responded by taking him down to the back of his throat.

God, if anybody knew time was limited and life was uncertain, it should be Damien, right? He'd taken a client into the air and his client had needed to rescue *him*.

He had a moment here, to taste, to touch, to "appreciate" this man who had insisted they deepen their connection. It was high time Damien learned that a good thing like this might not last forever.

He would taste this moment, this happiness, while it lasted.

Least Favorite Animal

"WE'RE late," Preston muttered.

"Sorry," Damien said. He didn't mean that—
Preston was getting better at knowing that sound in
Damien's voice, that look on his face.

"You are not," Preston corrected.

Damien paused at the corner of a very slow, dusty
street and regarded Preston with a look that could only
be classified as "amused." "Are you?" he asked.

Preston remembered what had made them late and
smiled. "Not even a little." He lowered his hand to where
Preacher stood, waiting for the cues that would send him
across the street. "But we'd better not tell Glen we were
late because you wanted to suck my—"

Damien flailed, his eyes growing large and frightened
for the first time that day, and Preston was sorry.

"Not so loud in public, Preston! There might be children around! Or assholes! Or perfectly ordinary people who don't want to know what we were doing twenty minutes ago!"

"Glen used to say that stuff around me all the time," Preston told him, and Damien shook his head, looking appalled. Preston thought that expression was Damien's funniest—he knew all the bad stuff Damien had done when he and Glen had been younger, and Damien being shocked by something Glen or Preston said was hilarious.

"Well, your brother's an asshole. Don't be that asshole, Preston. Remember to talk about that stuff—"

"Sex," Preston clarified.

"Sex, talk about it with an inside voice. Between you and me, okay?" Damien's face relaxed, and Preston could see a little bit of happiness and a little bit of sorrow mixed together, and he didn't know what to do with that look.

"It was between you and me," Preston said, forgetting they were late for a minute. "It was wonderful between you and me."

"Yes," Damien admitted readily, surprising him. "It was really wonderful."

Preston narrowed his eyes. "You sound like we're never doing it again. Is that why we had the... the thing twenty minutes ago? Because we're definitely doing it again, and we could have been on time."

"We need to go rescue Glen," Damien said, which wasn't an answer. "And it's going to be a while before we get anything resembling a bed again. Buddy's going to be eating, and we're going to want breakfast ourselves. He'll be okay waiting."

Oh, Preston didn't hear the important thing in that speech *at all*. "That's not an answer," he said, feeling his angry face snapping down like a garage door.

"I'm just saying that the next few days are going to be challenging," Damien said. "Come on, let's cross."

The town was small—a brisk twenty-minute walk from end to end sort of small. Most of the cars were American make, around ten years old. A *whole* lot of trucks, and pavement that was cracked from apathy or heat.

Relatively few people moved in that heat, which Preston could understand. He had trouble thinking in the heat, and Damien was making him grumpy. A block away, a woman in a flowered dress had her child by the hand to visit the drug store, and that was rush hour.

The block next to them had apparently been hit hard by the earthquake—a couple of the buildings had tumbled in and were marked with yellow tape, and none of the businesses were open. But Buddy had told them there'd been no casualties in Las Varas, and the few major injuries were being cared for in the hospital near Puerto Vallarta. Glen's supplies weren't needed here, but some help rebuilding would probably be appreciated.

As they crossed the street, Preston thought he could live here, except there weren't enough dogs. Besides, he liked where he lived *now*. In fact, it would be *perfect* if he could only get Damien to see reason and live there with him too.

"Well, after the next few days, we're still going to do that again, right?" Preston insisted when they were done crossing.

Damien looked at him, the unhappiness on his face so clear he might have written "doubtful" on his forehead in Sharpie. "Sure. We'll do it a couple of times, and then you'll get tired of my hours and decide there's someone better close to home. And then I'll be alone at night wishing I had a different job, any job, that would let me sleep with you more than once a week, and you'd be with someone else. And I'd remember the reason I do what I do and decide that it would never have worked. But we'll definitely do it again."

"If you're trying to read our fortune, you're doing it wrong," Preston told him. "For one thing, I don't mind being alone. You know that. So if you have to be gone a few nights a week, I'm okay. For another, you have *the exact* job that lets you stay with me more nights than that. You *ride a helicopter to work*. God, people say *I'm* thick."

Damien made a sort of laugh that sounded like he got his tongue stuck next to his nose, and Preston glared at him.

"You *are* thick," Damien said in an inside voice, and now Preston had to smirk because it was a dick joke, and who wouldn't laugh? Also, it was true.

"Yes, I am," Preston said proudly. "But you're thick in the head. You can fix your job—either you can do something else or you can love what you do now. You can fix where you live—because you know how to fly. And you're lucky. I didn't get my driver's license until I was twenty-one because I don't process information that quickly. If I flew, I'd kill us in a minute—crash, boom, explode! No more us! Your leg is your leg; it will get better or it won't. You work it and stretch it and do your best. What you can't fix, you live with. But the rest of it, you can fix. If you don't want to fix it so we can be together, that's fair, but be honest. That's a 'Damien doesn't want me' thing, not a 'Damien can't have me' thing."

Damien was just staring at him, mouth open, blinking rapidly.

"What?"

"That's a lot to take in," Damien said, his voice so strange Preston didn't even bother to try to decode it.

Well, not for *Preston*, but he'd learned a long time ago that not everybody thought like he did. "And?"

"You missed some things."

Preston thought hard, and realized that there was… a block. A wall. He'd seen that wall before—when Ozzy had decked him in the tenth grade, he'd felt that wall. When Damien had told him they couldn't have sex after his grandmother's funeral, he'd seen it looming.

There was a wall between what he saw and what Damien saw. But Damien had always been so good at explaining what was on the other side of the wall. Preston trusted him to show what he couldn't see.

"What did I miss?"

"That there are 'Damien is worried' things, or 'Damien doesn't know how to do relationships' things. And neither of these things means I don't *want* you—it just makes it harder for me to be with you and not be afraid."

"I can help you not be afraid," Preston said hopefully, but then his hope fell. "But I'm not good at relationships either. It's why I want one with you so bad. You show me what I'm missing instead of getting mad at me because I can't see."

Damien let out a breath and then, much like Preston reached down automatically to touch Preacher's head, he took Preston's hand in a gesture so automatic, so without thought, it gave Preston great joy.

"Whether last night happens again or not," Damien said, "I'll always be the guy who does that for you."

"But it would be better for both of us if we kept fucking," Preston reminded him, because that was the important thing.

Damien's eyes narrowed, and he dropped Preston's hand. "Unbelievable."

"What?" Preston asked, but Damien shook his head.

"You're relentless, and I'm hungry." He paused outside a small diner with a painting of a very confused-looking chicken and the caption El Pollo Delirante. "Let's get an egg burrito and find your brother."

"I'll have two eggs, scrambled, and wheat toast," Preston said, because that's what he had every morning. "No spice, no sausage, nothing different. Coffee." They pushed through the door into a small, neat, yellow-painted interior with white tile on the floor and clean Formica tables. The air-conditioning was blasting, and Preston felt himself relax with the temperature change. God, the next couple of days were going to suck.

"Understood." Damien searched his face, but eye contact was suddenly beyond him. "There's a corner table. Your tablet's charged."

Preston nodded. "Thank you," he said, that need to be alone and settled in his own head almost undoing him. This wasn't his place. Belinda made him the same breakfast every morning, and he sat at the table and played on his tablet, arranging his mind into neat little lines and columns before he planned his day. His grandmother had done the same thing. Before Glen had brought home the tablet, Preston had done number games—sudoku had been his favorite—and he still had clean paper books of little number grids in case the tablet died. The very first time he'd taken the dogs on a trip, he'd forgotten his sudoku pads and had been almost nonverbal by the time Patsy had guided him to his grandmother, so distraught he'd forgotten all of the things he'd learned about taking the dogs on a training run. His mother, his grandmother, and later Glen and Damien, had helped him develop and perfect the small, meaningful scaffold that helped him communicate with people outside his immediate circle, and helped him deal with new and unusual situations.

He knew he might not get his breakfast tomorrow—he was prepared for that. He'd packed his favorite granola bars with that knowledge. But he was pretty sure Damien would give him ten minutes to play on the tablet or do his puzzles, because sometimes that one thing was all that let him function in a strange environment.

Preston sat down to de-stress, and Damien went to talk to Buddy, who had just been served an egg burrito that was—his words—bigger than a horse's johnson. Preston sized up the burrito with his eyes and decided that was a lie to make Damien laugh, and then started his game, grateful for the small bit of routine.

Dealing with Damien was challenging—all of Preston's communication centers apparently needed to be engaged at all times. Damien's face, his voice, his words, his touch—all of it demanded his attention. The gain of Damien's sex was worth the extra work, but Preston needed to recharge his batteries or he'd forget his words.

He wasn't sure how long he lost himself in the simple game on his tablet. Food magically appeared on his table, and he ate it, comforted by the familiar taste, by the small part of routine, and of course, by Preacher at his feet. He finished his toast and frowned at his plate.

"There's sausage," he said. He actually liked sausage, but not for breakfast.

"That's for Preacher," Damien said from the counter.

Preston glanced at him and saw he was eating chorizo, beans, and eggs, using a tortilla in the same way Preston had used his toast to mop up his plate. He and Buddy were poring over a paper map, deep in discussion, probably about the route they'd be taking to where Glen's cell phone still beeped.

At Preston's feet, Preacher shifted slightly, his eyebrows lifting hopefully, as though he didn't know exactly who the sausage was meant for.

Preston broke the two links into small pieces and fed him, warning him that sausage wasn't an everyday occurrence, and he'd better be perfectly okay with kibble and dog treats after this. Preacher took the sausage from his fingers with a gentle mouth, licking the last of the grease off, just to be thorough, and Preston fondled his ears in return.

It occurred to him that Damien had ordered food for Preacher without needing words—or even a thank-you.

He crossed his knife and fork on his plate and pushed it aside, then finished the last of his coffee, feeling refreshed, almost as if he'd had a nap, which was silly because he'd slept *very* well the night before, wrapping Damien in safety.

Apparently Damien kept *him* safe from some things too.

That was never more apparent than when Damien squeezed his shoulder. "Ready to go?" he asked. "Buddy and I have a plan. Do you want to ride in back with Preacher?"

"The bill—"

"Paid it." Damien winked. "Quietest date I ever had."

Preston nodded and stood, turned his tablet off, and slid it into the reinforced case in his duffel. It should have seemed silly to Damien, hauling a delicate piece of electronics across the mountains on horseback, not to mention the small sudoku books. Not practical, Preston told himself. Not practical at all. But Damien took it in stride, gave him his morning headspace, offered him more time in the truck bed with Preacher.

"Do we have any idea where Glen is?" he asked, figuring that was what Damien and Buddy had been discussing while he'd been in his quiet zone.

"Location of his phone hasn't changed—he's outside of Agujero en la Roca, which is literally a hole in the rock in the middle of the mountains. I'm going to hazard a guess that this whole mess has something to do with that really big mansion with all the gardens, but...."

Damien bit his lip, obviously still gnawing on that problem.

"What's the matter?" Preston asked, wishing he could have been there in spirit for the conversation. Buddy led the way as they left the diner, and his truck was parked right around the corner. "Where's the horses?"

"They should be trailered in Buddy's pasture," Damien said. "Since that's on our way, we'll stop and pick them up. And as for what's the matter? I don't know. I asked Buddy—there's no drug cartels or anything unsavory out in that area, not that he's heard of. But he *has* heard of a sort of... I don't want to say cult or anything scary like that. Let's just say *gathering* of people, outside of Agujero en la Roca. A retreat. It's... it's disquieting that Glen's been somewhere that should have power, at least a generator, for so long, but hasn't texted us since yesterday. And it's really disquieting that this Cash kid led him such a merry chase. I don't know what it spells out, but I'm really anxious to get there."

"We can make it by tonight?" Preston asked, his own anxiety churning in his stomach. He couldn't read the same cues Damien could—and he believed Damien when he said he couldn't name what he was worried about. Damien and Glen were forever getting "hunches." Before the crash, Damien had been turning around in the helicopter because of a "hunch," and maybe the turn had saved his life.

"Not tonight," Damien muttered. "The terrain is rough even though the mountains aren't steep; it's rocky, there's drop-offs, the occasional snake or scorpion. It's easier not to step somewhere dangerous—or lead a horse somewhere dangerous—when you can see. Besides, we're going up in altitude, and that's rough going for man and beast. Better to find Glen and bring the supplies and figure out what he needs."

Preston nodded reluctantly. Damien made sense, and neither of them was afraid of rough going. In order to be certified to handle dogs in emergency situations, you had to go on forty-eight hour survivalist treks—two days to keep the dogs alive, keep yourself alive, and find your target. Preston did one of those every six months, usually carrying food for Preacher and whatever other dog he was training at the time. He knew better than to go wandering around at night. Most of the lost people he was sent to find had done that exact same thing.

"Don't want Preacher to have to find us," Preston said. "Especially when he'll be with us and not the rescue people."

Damien laughed, and it was time to hop into the truck and let the howl of the wind in his ears soothe his scrambled nerves.

THE next few hours were actually restful. Once they hooked the trailer up behind the truck, the bulk served as sort of a wind block. The terrain was flat until it hit the mountains and, unless there was irrigation and farmland, dry and scorched. Damien gave Preston his duffel, Preston pulled out his baseball cap, and he copped a nap on top of the bedroll and the horse blankets in the back of the truck. When they got to the trail at the base of the mountains, he and Preacher were more than ready for some physical activity.

Buddy parked in a turnabout before the trail narrowed to a four-foot axle-breaker that wound between trees and rocks. Damien took charge of the horses, belting the saddlebags and the travois on the pack animal, making sure the straps on the riding pads were not too tight, but not too loose. Buddy's saddles were soft and worn—but with more structure than a bareback pad alone. Damien and Preston both wore hiking boots, which, while not ideal, at least had reinforced steel toes in case the damned horse (Buddy's appellation) decided to dance on their feet.

The packhorse's travois had small all-terrain rubber wheels, but it extended a ways beyond her back end, so Preston heeded the reinforced requirement that she had to bring up the rear.

"Who are our horses?" Preston asked as Damien inspected the horses' hooves, using a small hoof pick that he'd pulled from a kit Buddy had given him to pull out any matter in the frog of the foot.

"This one's Chewie," Damien said, solidly patting the exceptionally large horse he was inspecting on the hindquarters. "He's a gelding and a moose, but Buddy here says he's exceptionally docile and follows SnakeEyes over there with a slavish devotion. SnakeEyes is mine, and she's apparently a real bitch."

"She has her moments," Buddy conceded, giving the packhorse its own inspection. "But you know what you're doing. I wouldn't trust her with someone inexperienced, and she's got good trail legs. If you were riding her alone, you could do this fifty-mile bit in a couple of hours, a week running, provided she has some rest and some good grub when she's done."

"Who's that?" Preston asked, nodding at the swaybacked mare who was carrying the supplies Glen had demanded.

"That's Sunshine," Buddy said, patting the mare's neck. "She's the sweetest little filly I've ever raised. Built like a house of sticks and uncomfortable as hell to

ride, but mostly she's like a really big dog. You give her
the right cues, you tell her where she's going, and she'll
do it all for you and expect nothing but an attagirl."
Buddy reached into his pocket and pulled out a green
cake of alfalfa, then broke a piece of it off for her. She
lipped it and nuzzled his shoulder, and he gave the
horse a completely unselfconscious kiss on her velvety
nose. "Attagirl," he mumbled.

Preston smiled. He and Sunshine could be friends.

"Here," Buddy told him, pulling a fanny pack from
around his waist. "Damien has one of these—it's got a
Leatherman, first aid kit, some nylon line for fixing tack,
a couple of granola bars in case you lose your supplies, a
bandana and safety pins for fuck-all whatever you want,
sunblock, saddle ointment, and a few other notions.
Keep it around your waist. This is all the shit that you
may wish you had but didn't think to bring. There's a
hook here on the saddle. Give me your duffel and I'll
attach it. Nice, not too heavy, that's good."

"Does Sunshine have food for us?" Preston asked,
because it had been a good four hours since breakfast.

"I've got some sandwiches for you boys in the
car, but Sunshine has a couple days' rations, don't you
worry. She's even got a bag of apples—but be sure you
share the cores. And don't let the other horses eat them
when you're not paying attention."

"I won't," Preston said soberly. He liked apples.

"And here." Buddy took out another small plastic
bag, this one filled with alfalfa cubes. "The horses will
graze, but the cubes have extra vitamins and some carbs
that will help sustain them if you have to press them
for speed. I'm tucking this in your bag—don't forget,
though, don't bring anything into the mountains that
you don't pack out, and be sure to dig your privy hole

deep. Sunshine's got the camp shovel there. Life gets hard without one, so try not to lose it, okay?"

Preston nodded again, glad his memory was good. Damien probably knew all these things, and Preston had been told them before, but a refresher course never hurt when you were about to get on the back of a ton of panicky animal that had an eye on either side of its face.

"You're not afraid of the horse, are you, son?" Buddy asked. "The last thing you want to do is get on the back of a horse when you're afraid."

"Horses don't see in three dimensions, and they've got a blind spot wider than a car up to ten feet in front of their face," Preston told him, his animal husbandry courses fresh in his mind. "One eye sees one thing, the other eye sees the other, and they can't adjust their focus because their own head's in the way. They can miss things—they can look at a field with a clothesline six thousand times and only see the clothesline on the six thousand and first. It startles them. You *think* the horse is seeing the same thing you are, but suddenly things are popping out in 3-D on them, and they get very upset. I'd get upset if my ranch had an entire secret life too, so you can't blame them. But it makes them… very unpredictable."

"Not a bad explanation," Buddy conceded. "And you're right. Horses are prey animals, and all they have is their ability to rear up and the ability to run. But *you* can see, so it's *your* job to tell that horse that clothesline is just a damned clothesline and not a threat. Once you get on the horse's back, he thinks you're in charge, so he does what you say. If you panic, he panics. If you tell him what he's supposed to be doing like you mean it, you two will be fine."

Preston approached Chewie from the left side and put both hands on the saddle. "I'm going to get on

you now, Horse. I expect you to behave." He put all
the assurance he had into those words, focusing on the
animal and nothing but the animal.

Chewie flicked his ears back and took a step forward,
right when Preston was about to hoist himself over. He
took a step back and scowled, reaching for Buddy's hand
so he could take the bridle himself. Firmly—but not
cruelly, because it *was* an animal—he pulled the horse's
head around so they could make some eye contact.

"Not funny. Now stay put." With that, he kept the
reins in that hand while he grasped the saddle pommel
and tried again.

Chewie stayed put, and he was immediately
overwhelmed with the smell of horse. Wonderful. He
was on top of a thousand-pound animal and would have
to stay there for the next two hours, until they got down,
gave everybody a drink of water, and then did it again.

"Good job," Damien praised, organizing the kit at
his waist. Had he packed that, Preston wondered, or did
Buddy have a spare one? He probably kept it in the
plane. God, Damien was good at stuff. At horses.

At everything.

"Preston, here!" Buddy passed him up a packet
wrapped in a small cloth bag, and as Preston sat, keeping
as still as he could, he looked inside and saw two cheese
sandwiches on hearty wheat bread, an apple, and a
refillable collapsible canteen. "Lunch!"

Preston took a breath, and the horse remained mostly
still. "Thank you," he said sincerely. Things would feel
more doable after food. He ate while Damien finished his
check of the horses and gear, and looked around carefully,
getting accustomed to the quiet movements of Chewie
under him.

Buddy had brought the truck and the trailer through much of the foothills on a narrow mountain road. He'd pulled off while he still had room to back up and turn around, at a place where the horses had some flat road before the whole thing narrowed into a trail. The climate here was close to tropical—what was a dusty and dry June in northern California was an uncomfortable, humid summer here at the base of the mountains. Preston knew that the farther inland they went into the mountains, the drier and rockier it would get, but he figured they had a good three days riding before they were in Zacatecas and things got really crispy, and they'd reach the Agujero en la Roca before that. Far away he heard the rush of water, and figured they were closer to the Grande de Santiago—perhaps Damien planned to stop and water their horses in a tributary.

Either way, Preston was grateful for the canteen of water, still cool, and the sandwiches. Buddy gave Damien a similar packet, and tucked a Ziploc into Damien's saddlebags that contained antibiotics and heavy-duty painkillers in case the situation was dire. Damien took his lunch and flashed Preston a grin.

"You can eat both of yours," he said as he looped the packet around the saddle horn. Preston looked at his own, looped around his wrist and tangling with the reins, and followed Damien's lead.

So many things here he didn't know.

And that was it. Damien put one hand on the horse's ass, grabbed the pommel with the other, and swung himself gracefully up into the saddle. He looked behind him and smiled encouragingly at Preston.

"Now you don't have to post, but it will save your ass and your spine if you do. These are Western trained horses. Lift yourself off the saddle on every third beat, remember?"

"I remember that that's never as easy as it sounds," Preston said sourly, and Damien winked, as though he understood.

"My leg's aching just thinking about it," he said in complete candor, and Preston grimaced. He needed to remember that not everything was easy for Damien— no matter how smooth he made it look.

"I'll do my best," he said, trying to absorb Damien's goodwill and make it his own.

"You got your sat phone charged?" Damien called to Buddy before he got to the truck.

"I do. I'll be twenty miles away from this spot. You saw that little town, right?"

Preston remembered it vaguely. It had been mostly a gas station and a diner, with a couple of power charging stations and a liquor store.

"I do," Damien said. "So you're camping out there for a couple of days?" His voice grew crisp and military. This was the way he and Glen spoke when they were talking about mission-critical matters. It was funny how he could go so serious, when much of what made Damien was laughter.

"Till I hear from you otherwise," Buddy told him. "Be sure to tag me if you need more supplies too. I got a report this morning that some of the hilltop towns were nearly leveled, and the river's been flooding with aftershocks. Keep your wits about you, even if you're just at a low point in the river, you hear me?"

"Loud and clear. Thanks, Buddy. We'll give you a ping when we find our guys. Or, you know, scream for you to bail our asses out of the fire."

Buddy laughed. "I live for that call, you know it. Be safe, you two."

One more wave and they were on their way.

Preston was afraid Damien would take off at a canter, but he didn't. He set the horses at a walk and checked Preston's form, offering him advice and encouragement, showing him tricks to hold himself upright on the horse. Preston's core and legs were strong. Damien kept telling him to use what he had, and in spite of the sweat trickling down his spine, Preston started to feel a little more comfortable and a little less like the next fifty miles might be a terrible sacrifice for the brother he loved.

Chewie was a sweet animal, but as Preston had learned, arguing with Damien, sweet didn't mean "will do everything you want without question." Their path—and the trail they were following—led southwest, inland and up the mountains, but it was the hardest way to go.

"Dammit! Stop trying to go downhill!" Preston burst out about a half an hour in. "What do I have to do?"

"Be relentless," Damien called, his best, most brilliant grin crossing his face. "You know, same way you talked me into bed!"

Preston stared at him for a moment, outraged, and then he realized Damien was teasing him. "You don't seem sorry," he said, trying to gauge how true that was.

Augh! Another look Preston couldn't fathom. It was like Damien had sprouted a whole new host of expressions since their conversation the day before, and Preston had to plow through the weeds of Damien's errant emotions before he got to the truth.

"Are you?" Damien asked, and Preston snorted.

"Are you serious?" He'd been reliving the night before during the truck ride, every moment of it playing back in his head like his favorite movie. And then, when the credits had rolled on that, he thought about that morning, when Damien had come to him. Had initiated their touching, stroked Preston's thighs, pulled Preston's cock into his sweet mouth because he'd wanted to taste.

It had been everything Preston had ever dreamed about their coming together—with the exception of Preston's dumb-shit brother being missing so they had to leave the hotel room to come ride a one-ton idiot animal.

"Never mind," Damien said, turning away.

"Really?" Preston so didn't get people. "You're going to have this conversation when—*dammit, Chewie, I said don't go there!*" He gave a tug of the reins in frustration, and the horse, contrary to everything he'd done previously, went exactly where Preston had indicated and even cantered a little to catch up to Damien and SnakeEyes.

Now Damien was looking over his shoulder and laughing. "Well, you've managed to master the horse, at least."

Preston was done with wordplay. "I mastered you too," he said shortly. "I told you—that's not our last time. And the next time won't be the last time, and the time after that won't be the last time. Do you want me?" He didn't mean just for sex, but he was *on the back of a horse*, and he could only do one thing at a time.

"Yes," Damien said, and thank God for a straight answer. Damien and Glen could take their words and shove them up a horse's ass.

"Then we will find a way to be together." Chewie tried to stop, because apparently there was a tuft of grass that had to be eaten right now. "Sometime when we're *not* riding these idiot animals!"

Damien burst out laughing. "Idiot animals?"

"My dogs are smarter," Preston said resentfully.

"Very probably," Damien told him, "but a horse is not a dog."

"Thank God," Preston said with feeling. Augh! Fuck this horse and fuck this heat! "Because then it would be a gigantic fucking idiot dog!"

"Not a bad way to describe a horse, really," Damien said, patting the side of his mount's neck. "But I like them."

Preston had the feeling Damien was amused. Well, Preston might *be* amusing, but Damien was apparently not leaving him behind. Not even on horseback, where Preston really did not want to be.

"It wasn't a one-time thing," Preston reiterated. God, look at Damien, smiling, graceful, considerate, and yes, tough. Tough enough to haul them through the mountains of Nayarit to find Preston's asshole brother. Tough enough to come back from a helicopter crash that probably would have scared Preston enough to keep him grounded for life.

Tough enough to go up in the air almost daily, when it still scared him.

Whatever Damien thought of the night before, of this conversation, of their future, Preston needed him to acknowledge this. Their being together wouldn't go away. If Preston could make the idiot horse do what he needed it to, Damien should have the good sense to go the way Preston needed *him* to without jerking on any reins.

Damien grinned at him, his body as fluid on the horse as he used to be in the air, his perfect mouth turned up at the corners. "If I concede to that, are you ready to pick up speed?" he said.

Preston looked around for Preacher and saw him a few feet ahead on the trail, looking like he could run easily for at least an hour.

"Sure," Preston said. "Let's make some time."

The quicker they got to Glen, the quicker they'd get home and Preston could see what noises Damien would make when he wasn't afraid people would hear.

THE break they took in two hours wasn't long enough. Preston could barely move as he swung himself off Chewie's back, and his ass felt like it had sweated through his shorts to stick to the saddle. The horse had apparently learned who was boss during their first stint, though, because he stood docilely and allowed Preston to lead him to the muddy shore of the tributary where Damien had already brought Sunshine and SnakeEyes.

Damien drank deeply from his canteen, and then, to Preston's surprise, pulled out a little testing kit for the water in the stream, staring at the results for a minute before shaking his head.

"We'll have to use some of Sunshine's bottled water for now," he said, pulling out another, larger soft-sided bottle to fill. "We can filter and boil this tonight and use it to fill up all the bottles."

"What's wrong with it?" Preston looked at the three different papers that Damien had dipped into the sample he'd taken.

"Pesticides and E. coli," Damien told him. "The E. coli won't affect the horses, and the pesticides are light enough for the moment, but we'll want to give them fresh water tomorrow. Sometimes when there's an earthquake, bacteria is stirred up from the bottom of a water source, and sometimes things that are stored nearby break and filter into the water. This is flowing down into the Grande de Santiago. I think there's a small dam upstream and a filtration plant, so whatever is here is new, probably less than fifty miles or so."

"You're thinking the pesticide is from those gardens you saw in the satellite," Preston deduced.

Damien shrugged. "It's a possibility. Just makes me curious." He pushed himself up from his squat by the stream and grunted, his face screwing up in pain.

"What?" Preston asked. "What hurts?"

Damien grunted. "My leg," he said shortly. Then he pulled a strained smile that Preston knew was for his benefit. "My *ass*," he added, like he was trying to be funny.

"Does your ass really hurt?" Preston had wondered—somewhat guiltily—if getting on the back of a horse was such a good idea after their activity the night before.

"A little," Damien conceded. "But not as bad as my leg after being on a horse." He took a deep breath and fished out a familiar plastic bottle of over-the-counter pain medication, which he washed down with water from his canteen.

"I can rub your leg," Preston told him, thinking that Damien probably had to be in a *lot* of pain to admit to feeling a little.

"Two more hours," he said, looking at the sky. "Two more hours, we can take a slightly longer break, and then after another hour we can make camp. It won't get dark until late tonight. We can make up a lot of ground."

Preston stretched his body from feet to fingertips and tried to suppress a groan. Everything hurt, and he was sweating like a sponge. "Horses," he said darkly. "My brother has a lot to answer for."

Damien smiled slightly and then pulled a surprise out of the food bag that Buddy had given him. "Here— have some. It'll cheer you up."

He opened a large can of trail mix and offered Preston a handful. Preston took a bite and munched, the sweetness easing his worry a little. "We can eat our apples at the next stop," he said.

"I think the horses will appreciate that greatly."

Damien, standing so close, smiling and relaxed—and happy, for all the pain he must have been in—was just so… so damned pretty. For a moment there was only that smile, the sound of the stream, and the hot wind coming down from Zacatecas smelling of pine and oak and creosote bush.

But mostly pretty Damien.

Preston leaned into Damien's body, hoping he was reading the quiet moment right. "I want to kiss you now," he said softly. "Don't startle."

Damien's eyes went wide and his lips parted, and Preston paused for a moment, because that could have been surprise and that could have been yes, and he needed to know it was yes.

"Okay," Damien whispered. "You can kiss me now."

Their lips touching under the sunshine were almost as sweet as trail mix. Preston tasted him enough for Damien to be the dessert, and not the nuts and chocolate.

Preston pulled away from the kiss, breathing surprisingly fast. It was like he could taste Damien's laughter, his sweetness, just from his lips. "I always want more," he complained.

"Yeah. Me too."

Preston beamed at him. "Excellent."

Damien's soft laugh was their signal to start packing up.

Over Hill

DAMIEN'S leg was on fire, and it was weak enough that every other part of his body was burning in sympathy, particularly his stomach, back, and other leg.

His ass was a little sore—that was the truth—but the burning of his weakened leg was painful enough that he couldn't hide it at their second rest stop, and Preston was the one who called a halt to their final ride of the day.

"I can hear you," he muttered, after telling Damien to stop. "You're making these little grunting sounds every time you post. It hurts me to listen. Get off the horse and let me make camp."

"Fine," Damien muttered. "I'll take care of the horses." Preston had put on a good face, and he seemed to have reached a rapport with his mount—and he'd relaxed considerably as the temperature had dropped—

but SnakeEyes was, in fact, piss mean, just as Buddy had warned. She'd tried to take a piece of Damien a couple of times, and part of the reason Damien's leg hurt so bad was that she'd been actively working to throw him. He'd had to put a lot of pressure into his knees and thighs to show her who was boss, and the effort had taken its toll.

"Are we going to tie them to a tree or something?" Preston asked, searching their clearing nervously. The ground was dusty, and scorched grasses made up the ground cover under the pine and oak of the mountains.

Damien held up a hand and listened, hearing the tributary that had run roughly parallel to their trail tinkling about twenty yards away.

"Let's make our way to the stream," he said thoughtfully. "The horses can drink, and maybe we can find a place to make a fire pit where the grasses won't threaten to catch in the slightest breath of wind."

"And we can tie them to a tree," Preston repeated, glaring at Chewie while the horse munched dry grass at Preston's feet.

"We can tie SnakeEyes to a tree," Damien muttered, glaring at his mount, who glared back. "The others won't want to leave once she's settled. Come on, let's find a good camp before night falls. I don't want to suddenly find a rattler or something who's not excited about making friends."

Preston grunted. "We have snakes on the ranch," he said, which didn't surprise Damien. He'd seen plenty of them while working the property with Glen in their younger years.

"I know it. You still hiring a wrangler when you can?"

"Yeah, but sometimes they're just close up to the dogs, you know?"

Killing snakes always struck him as cruel and pointless, unless they were a direct threat to man or livestock. They were truly awesome animals, but they could be really dangerous too.

"I know," Damien consoled, taking SnakeEyes's reins in one hand and Sunshine's in the other. "Let's go make sure we don't have to kill a snake now."

They found a flat spot that was all clear, with enough river rock nearby to build a fire pit. Damien left Preston to that job while he rubbed the horses down with a cloth from his saddlebags, then brushed them and picked their feet. One misplaced pebble could reduce their giant, graceful modes of transportation to a giant, treacherous liability. Damien had to keep the horses healthy or his and Preston's quest to bring back Glen was doomed.

By the time he was done tending them, his hands were shaking with exhaustion and pain. Preston appeared at his elbow, escorting him to the small fire he'd started, and he helped him settle down on a fallen tree.

Damien looked around at the rapidly encroaching night, the small campfire, even the makeshift seat, and gave a dry chuckle.

"What?" Preston asked, stirring some soup in a tin pot that he'd rigged over the fire.

"Last time I roughed it like this, I was in a snow shelter and Mal and Tevyn were trying to keep me alive."

Preston grunted. "What did they do?"

"I was pretty out of it, but when my leg got infected, Mal almost died getting firewood. Tevyn was busy making poultices, I guess, and he looked up and realized Mal had fallen in a hole and decided to take a nap. Scared them both pretty bad."

Preston gave a deep sigh. "I'm so jealous of them," he said. "And yes, I know. It's irrational. I wanted to be there. I wanted to rescue you. And the guy you'd been crushing on rescued you instead. And then we got back and the three of you were your own little club, and you only smiled with them. It wasn't fair."

Damien regarded him quietly, watching as he stood and dished the stew into two plastic bowls that had been in the kit on Sunshine's back. Preston handed him a bowl and a spoon, and Damien took a bite. It was lukewarm, but that was okay—he was starving. Preston had probably pulled it early so he could put the biggest pot on the fire to boil water for the morning. They ate in silence for a moment, but that didn't mean Damien wasn't thinking about what he said.

After a few bites, he patted the tree he was sitting on. "Come sit."

"Why?" Preston asked, but he was moving.

"So I can lean against you."

Preston laughed and did as asked, taking Damien's weak side. "Finish your food, and I'll rub your leg, just like you rubbed down the horses," he said, and Damien nodded, tired and in pain and not willing to argue. It was like last night. Preston wanted to take care of him, and he was warm and strong, and Damien trusted him to do that.

"I miss horseback riding. I should do it more often. The leg might heal faster."

"Why don't you?" Preston asked, putting his hand, warm and capable, on Damien's thigh. He squeezed slightly, and Damien felt some of the tension drain from his shoulders, like the night before.

"Busy," Damien mumbled. "Keeping the business afloat. We keep getting new clients."

"You guys should hire someone else," Preston said, making more sense than Glen or Damien ever did, truth be told.

"You and your logic," Damien said, laughing a little. Preston increased the pressure, kneading at a knot in his lower thigh. "Yeah. It gets… lost, in the daily demands, I guess. This was supposed to be our weekend. I had to turn Mal and Tevyn over to another contractor to be here."

"Why'd Glen take the contract to find this kid, then?" Preston set his bowl down on the tree and moved in front of him to concentrate both hands on Damien's calf, and for a moment Damien's vision blurred, the relief was so acute.

"Couldn't tell you," Damien said, and that was the truth. "We were going to spend two days by the pool, ordering takeout." He yawned. "I miss that plan."

Preston paused. "But then we wouldn't have had sex. Are you sorry?"

Damien blinked and took a breath. That was the second time Preston had asked, which meant he needed reassurance. He reached down and took Preston's hands in his own, rough and capable, and waited for Preston to make the eye contact he usually avoided.

There. Ah, there. Preston's eyes were even blue by firelight. So pretty and pure. Damien smoothed his thumbs over Preston's knuckles and did what he always had done with Preston—told the truth.

"No. I'm glad we…." He stumbled. He couldn't just say "had sex," because with Preston it felt so much larger than that. That's why Damien had avoided it for so long, and then been afraid of it for a little longer. "Made love," he finished, and this time he looked away. "I'm glad we did. I… I have no promises, Preston, except that I always want to be in your life. But I'm glad that… that for at least that perfect moment, we got to be together."

"Okay. Then we can do it again, and you won't be sorry." Preston smiled smugly, and Damien had to laugh.

"Okay," he said, conceding. His shoulders eased up, a weight of tension he didn't know he'd been carrying trickling away. Had he been worrying about how it would end? How he and Preston would *stop* being lovers and still continue to be friends? He must have been—that must have been what had been hanging on his neck all day. But Preston saw straight to the heart of things—he always had. And it was such an easy way to look—they would be together again. They both wanted it. It had made them happy.

As Preston's hands kept working their magic on Damien's leg and Damien sank further and further into his own spine, melting into the hard bark of the tree, he thought there were worse things in life than the thing that made him happy.

Preston left him a few moments later to rinse out their dishes and set up their bedrolls, and came back with the bowls to put in the pack on Sunshine's travois. The pan on the fire was boiling, and Preston set that one aside.

"I'm going to boil a second pot on the embers," he said. "That's not enough for the horses."

"Good idea." Damien yawned. "I'll stay up to keep an eye out until it dies completely."

Preston snorted. "No. Go brush your teeth, then lie down and make all your noises. I'll be there when you're ready."

Damien opened his mouth to protest, but Preston was already handing him a water bottle. Damien did as he was told, settling himself on his side so he could watch Preston prepare everything but the fire. There was something soothing about that big figure silhouetted against the brutally black night sky, doing simple domestic things to care for the both of them. He didn't want to close his eyes or he might miss the way Preston still looked like a fallen angel by firelight, or the sound the trees made when the wind hit them. Miss the smell of the campfire, or pine trees, or the earthiness of oak. Once upon a time, he'd loved camping. He didn't smell the salt and flowered perfume of Kahua Nui-Makai here, but waiting for Preston like this brought back that same joy.

He was dozing slightly when he heard Preston kicking dirt on the embers, and he shifted slightly as Preston came to the bedrolls and took off his boots. They used Damien's duffel as a pillow, and it wasn't until Preston positioned himself as the big spoon that Damien realized how much he'd depended on the idea of that big, solid body behind him. At their feet, Preacher *whuff*led and curled up near Damien's knees, and Damien gave half a laugh.

"What?" Preston asked, hand snugging around Damien's stomach.

"Think Preacher's going to be okay with me in his spot?"

"Keep feeding him sausage," Preston said with a yawn. "He'll love you most."

No. Preston would always be that dog's person. But as Damien listened to the unfamiliar sounds of the forest around them, Preacher's solid weight, Preston's warmth at his back, even the horses dozing contentedly near the water, gave him a strange sense of contentment, one he hadn't had since he was a child. His parents had loved him then, or he'd believed so. He hadn't seen the way that love lived and died by his grades, by his performance in swimming and polo. He hadn't seen the way his life had been scripted, his parents' approval the carrot on the end of an increasingly longer stick.

The look on his mother's face when he was twelve and told her he wanted to take out another boy in school had changed all that. The fights he'd had with his father about entering the armed forces so he could learn to fly had done the rest.

Here, under the open sky and the diamond-bright scattering of a million stars, he felt warm and sheltered.

Loved.

Which was usually a scary word when he was hooking up with a lover. Except Preston didn't put things in terms of emotions. He put things in terms of actions.

The action he wanted was to keep sleeping with Damien until they found a way to make the relationship work. It was such a simple plan, but the rewards... the rewards were Preston, his hands on Damien's skin in comfort, his no-bullshit conversation forcing Damien to stop screwing around and get to the point. And at the end of the day, it was Preston at his back, making him feel sheltered and warm for as long as they both shall live.

As Damien closed his eyes, he realized he could work toward a goal like that.

DAMIEN wasn't sure what woke him first—the shifting of the horses, the roar of the water, or maybe it was a vibration in the earth.

All he knew was that one minute he was asleep, the pain in his leg faded, Preston's solid warmth the only security he needed, and the next minute, he'd scrambled out of the bedroll amid Preacher's frantic barking.

"What?" Preston demanded as Damien checked his boots for critters before sliding them on and fumbling with the laces. "What? What is that noise?"

"The river," Damien muttered. "I can hear the river. Gather the stuff. I'm getting the horses—"

At that moment, Chewie and Sunshine came cantering out of the trees, because Damien hadn't tied them. "Load Sunshine," he said. "Settle Chewie's saddle. I'll be back."

He ran by starlight, mostly, glad in a way that he and Preston had refrained from breaking out flashlights. His vision was better in the light from the sky, and he could see the shadows of the trees in stark relief. SnakeEyes gave a rather frantic nicker, and Damien increased his pace. He didn't care how nasty the horse was, whatever was happening—

The roar of the water rolling down the hill cued him in first.

It was coming, like a wall, and as he skidded to a halt next to SnakeEyes, he shouted, "Preston! Hook up the travois and get everybody to higher ground!" before going to work on the reins he'd tied around a young tree. The mare didn't help him, not in the least. She tossed her head and pranced like a diva, until Damien pulled the Leatherman from the pouch he'd worn— even to bed—and used it to part the leather so he could undo the knot. He hissed at the shock of the cold as water started rising, up past the river bank, past his ankles, as he worked on the damned leather.

Finally it was free, and he swung up on the frantic horse's back, legs stiff from the chill, urging the mare to run, to swim, to leap over the rising water, because if they didn't get clear of that surge coming down the hill—

He looked under his arm and smacked SnakeEyes on the ass with what was left of the lead.

The water crashed through the trees not twenty feet behind them.

In a burst of speed worthy of a champion, SnakeEyes blew through the clearing to the camp, which was blessedly empty.

They'd camped in a small depression before the trail they'd been following continued to gain altitude, and Damien urged his mount up the hill, fast, faster!

The water thinned around the horse's ankles, then became a splashing under her shoes.

Right when he started worrying about where Preston had gone, the ground under her feet was puffing dust. He rounded a bend in the road just in time to watch Preston go flying off Chewie's back.

Preston landed on his face, his palm out to shield him, his shoulder taking much of the momentum, and his loud cry of "Ouch! Fuck!" drove Damien to his side.

"The hell?" he snapped, sliding off SnakeEyes's back and keeping her cut reins in his hand. "Preston, are you okay?"

Preston was struggling to sit up, but his wrist obviously pained him. Preacher whined and licked his face, and Damien could see his nose was streaming blood—not to mention the shredded skin on the bridge of it.

"Nose looks broken," he said softly. "Here, Preston, let me check. What happened?"

"I didn't tighten the saddle cinch enough," Preston mumbled through his streaming nose. "The saddle started to slide down, and I dropped the reins and grabbed his neck."

"And he stopped," Damien said, because that's what horses did when they thought they were losing their rider.

"And I couldn't hold on," Preston finished miserably. "Damien, I left your saddle and the bedroll at the site. I'm sorry. The water was coming and the horses were panicking. I got our duffels and the food, but…."

"It's me and the saddle pad for the rest of the trip," Damien concluded. "It's okay, Preston. You did great. You got everybody clear of the flood; you saved the supplies we're carting in. Don't worry, man. I'm not mad." God, in all that chaos, Preston had led two horses and himself to safety. The loss of the saddle would hurt—not to mention the heavy-duty medical supplies like oral antibiotics and injectable steroids that had been in the saddlebags—but not nearly as much as the loss of the horses.

Or Preston.

Preston nodded and closed his eyes, rocking back and forth gently to calm himself, holding the wrist that had blocked his fall at an angle. "I saved my duffel bag," he said. "My tablet's okay. My puzzles are okay. I have clean socks for tomorrow. I have a clean shirt for tomorrow. I have treats for Preacher for tomorrow."

It was obviously a ritual of sorts, to calm himself down, and Damien let him do that while he went to Sunshine to settle her and gather some gear. He came back to Preston with the first aid kit, and took some time wiping the gravel out of the scrapes on his face before putting ointment on, hoping he got everything in the dimness of starlight.

By the time he was done with that, Preston's nose had stopped bleeding and he'd stopped rocking himself, which was a good thing.

"Okay, I'm going to wrap a bandana around your wrist, okay?"

Preston nodded and yelped, and Damien grimaced. "Hold still for a second," he said softly, pushing his thumb along Preston's neck and collarbone on the side that had taken all of his weight. He hit a swollen spot and Preston let out another bark of discomfort.

"That's your collarbone," he said grimly. "Here— very carefully give me your sore wrist first."

Preston held out his corded forearm, his jaw locked at an angle as he dealt with the discomfort. Damien jerry-rigged a makeshift bandage using his bandana and the safety pins from his personal kit, and then pulled an ace bandage from the first aid kit he'd gotten from Sunshine.

"What are you doing with that?" Preston asked dolefully. He was obviously in pain and trying to deal, but Damien gave him a solid squeeze to the knee before he answered.

"I'm going to wrap a figure eight around your shoulders, to keep them back, and then a sling for your arm, so you don't aggravate your collarbone. It's going to hurt, but the bandage will help, okay?"

Preston nodded. "I'm no help at all," he moaned.

"Yeah, well, I've been there. I can tell you that just hanging in there and letting me treat you without complaining is a big plus, okay?"

"Okay," Preston muttered. "I won't complain."

Damien laughed. "You will too, but you'll also do your best, so that's okay too. Sometimes complaining helps pass the time."

"It's my brother's favorite hobby," Preston said darkly.

"Right? If bitching was an art form, Glen would get paid for making masterpieces, right?"

Preston breathed deeply as Damien put pressure on his shoulder. "If whining was a science, he would have discovered new life forms," he said, obviously enjoying this game.

Damien used to love games like this too. Like a blow came the memory of Glen telling him they were spending the weekend at the pool, getting drunk enough that Damien would finally fight back again, and the frozen feeling on Damien's face as he tried to smile and say "Sure." He swallowed and hoped Glen's ears were burning, because Damien needed a chance to play like this with his friend again. "Exactly. If kvetching was a profession, he'd be a billionaire."

Preston laughed at that one. "You know what he'd say to that, right?"

"He'd be damned if he got good at anything that made him rich?"

Another laugh. "Is that why you guys started the business? So you'd get rich?"

Damien paused. "Here, lift your arm," he said, and then finished securing the figure eight around his shoulders. "We started it so we could work with our brothers," he said after a moment. The three of them, doing the things they loved—that had been the plan. "So we could have fun doing something we loved and still help people."

Preston took a deep breath. "You'll love it again," he said softly.

Damien was glad they weren't looking at each other. It meant he didn't have to look away. "I'm so afraid I won't."

Preston tried to lift his good hand and winced when he realized that was his bad shoulder. "You will. If Preacher bit me, I'd be afraid, but I'd still have to love dogs."

Preacher stuck his head between them and licked Preston's face, like just hearing the idea that he could bite was upsetting.

"Then I'll have to love it," Damien said lightly. He'd grabbed one of the towels from Sunshine's pack and used his knife to split it into a giant triangle. He finished the sling and gently immobilized Preston's arm against his chest and then looked around and took stock.

They could hear the flood rushing in the lower level of their camp, but the water hadn't even snuck past the bend in the narrow trail. The horses were moving restively, and SnakeEyes was wet and shivering.

"Okay," Damien muttered. "Here's what I'm going to do."

He pulled off Chewie's saddle, which was hanging sideways and starting to freak the horse out a little anyway. When he was done he propped it up against a tree and helped Preston out of the road, setting him against the saddle like a chair back. Another trip to pull the horses all together, this time tying Chewie to a tree and hoping SnakeEyes was enough of a herd animal not to take off until he fixed her tack, and he grabbed one of the beach towels and rolled it up behind Preston's head. He snagged Preston's duffel from the middle of the road and pulled out his tablet and the battery and handed them to Preston. He could almost hear Preston's sigh of relief through the soles of his boots as Preston escaped from the pain and the confusion of the night into his comfort zone.

He unpacked Sunshine again, giving thanks that Buddy knew what he was doing. The towels, water, and food were easily accessible in their own packs, and each pack attached to the pack saddle with a minimum of fuss.

The horses settled and accounted for, he grabbed the one bedroll that had been hastily thrown over Sunshine's neck and limped over to Preston, tapping his feet respectfully.

Preston looked up after a moment, and Damien said, "We need to try this again."

Preston turned off the tablet and put it in the case in his duffel, and Damien spread the bedroll out from the saddle like the saddle was the pillow in the bed. Damien added the duffels that Preston had dropped when he'd fallen off Chewie and helped Preston settle down again for whatever sleep they could get.

"Wait!" Damien muttered, and grabbed the painkillers from his waist pouch. "You have the rest of the water?"

Preston nodded soberly and washed down the ibuprofen, and then patted the space next to him gingerly, careful of what was probably a break in his wrist.

"Your leg hurts," he said.

"Well, yeah, but you're the one with the broken wrist and collarbone," Damien said, sinking down carefully, leg extended. His shoes and socks were wet, but he wasn't ready to kick them off quite yet. For a moment, he simply sat and shivered, until Preston leaned against him.

"This is the second time I broke bones falling off a horse," he muttered.

"I'm sorry, baby." The endearment slipped out, but Preston didn't seem to notice.

"I think you're right—they're like really fuckin' stupid dogs."

Damien laughed softly. "I think that's a prejudice you'll never overcome." Preacher made his way to Preston's other side and whined softly, nuzzling the arm in the sling. Damien reached over Preston's body to reassure him.

"You still love them," Preston said, nuzzling Damien's hair in the same way Preacher was nuzzling his arm.

Damien thought about SnakeEyes and her determination to get clear of the flood, of the way her muscles bunched beneath his thighs. He thought of Sunshine's sweetness and Chewie's amicability, and how that afternoon, all three of the horses had about become their love slaves when they'd been given apples and apple cores as a treat.

"I really do," he said, watching the three friends touch noses to flanks and hindquarters, reassuring the others that all was well.

"We can get a horse for the ranch," Preston promised, nuzzling Damien's temple. "We can get two. Instead of quad-runners. You can teach me to ride on your days off. We can run the dogs across the fields. You could be happy."

Damien's eyes burned. Preston was hurt and scared, and to him, he'd just been betrayed by a thousand-pound idiot dog—again. But he was willing to give horses another chance if it would lure Damien to his ranch.

He turned a little and captured Preston's mouth briefly, careful of the broken nose, knowing they were both cold and frightened and still shaky from the adrenaline comedown, but wanting the earthy animal taste of him. He pulled back and said, "I could be happy without the horses, you know. If you and me could make it work, that would be all I need."

Preston let out a sigh not unlike Preacher's, as the dog flopped over Preston's thighs. "We should maybe get the horses anyway."

Damien laughed softly. "You'd be enough," he said, his voice so quiet he wasn't sure Preston heard him.

But Preston kissed his temple, and Damien rather thought he had.

He'd have to get up and take off his shoes, make a proper camp, double-check on the horses—he knew that. But his eyes closed, and he was warmed enough by Preston's body to be comfortable.

He woke up at dawn the next morning when one of the horses whickered, and sat up from using Preston's chest as a pillow to look around frantically, wondering what had happened when he'd dared to close his eyes.

Nothing. The horses were still gathered together in the chill of the dawn, near the biggest oak tree off the path. SnakeEyes was still missing a saddle, Preston was still injured, a couple of lovely black eyes blooming over his broken nose, and they were still fucked.

Preston gave a little grunt in his sleep, and Damien touched his chest and rubbed, amending that last part. He was grateful Preston had been able to forget about the pain and the panic of the night before. Grateful he'd escaped the water, and that neither he nor SnakeEyes had sprained or broken anything in their mad dash through the trees to the road.

Painfully, because his leg had frozen up overnight, Damien stretched out and rubbed Preston's chest just a little bit harder.

"Preston? Buddy, you awake?"

"I liked 'baby' better," Preston slurred.

So Damien tried it out, now that he wasn't panicked and worried. "Okay. Preston, *baby*, are you awake?"

"I am now because you woke me up," Preston grumbled. He made to sit up and yelped when he put too much weight on his wrist. "Shit."

"Yeah, okay. I need you to close your eyes for a minute."

Preston glared at him unhappily. "Why?"

"Because I've got to get up to help you up, and me getting up isn't going to be pretty. It's embarrassing, and I'd rather you not see." He said it matter-of-factly, but his shame was acute.

Preston's glare got worse. "Are you shitting me?"

Damien tilted his head back and tried stretching his leg again. *Augh! Everything hurts.* "No. Not shitting you. Please, man, you gotta let me have my pride."

"I can't move either one of my arms," Preston muttered. He tried to wrinkle his nose, but the scrapes on his face had set overnight, and his scowl actually bled. "You are *literally* going to have to wipe my bottom for me until I get a cast for my wrist. I want to see the show!"

Damien swore and went to his knees, propping his good one up, using the tree they were by to lean on until he could push up on one leg, then trying weight on his bad one. It was awkward and ungainly and—

"Is that all?" Preston demanded. "Oh my God. I'm going to have to teach the dogs to wipe my ass. If that's the only show I get to see, that's not nearly as bad as what I've got going."

Jesus. "If I find the dog wiping your ass, it's over between us," Damien snapped. "Now hang on a minute while I figure out how I'm going to get *you* up."

Preston rolled his eyes and pulled both feet underneath him, standing from a squat without much problem at all.

"That's disgusting," Damien muttered. "That's really disgusting."

"I spend most of my time running with the dogs," Preston said guilelessly.

"I don't even know if I'm talking to you."

"My thighs and calves are *really* well developed." Oh, that smug bastard.

"Just stand there and look pretty while I load and saddle the horses." Damien felt like sticking out his tongue, but that would be childish and wrong. He gave Preston a sour look as he set about his chores and was surprised by Preston's expression.

"What? What is that face?" He could swear it was Preston's sunshiniest smile.

"Damien's back," Preston said happily. "I missed him."

"I'm right here. Dying to find your brother so I can kick his ass."

"I'm so happy!" Preston said.

Damien couldn't help it. Before he set to work, getting their food out first, he grinned back. And winked.

Preacher Gets a Say

IT took them a while to get started. Damien actually had to sew his horse's reins back together because he'd apparently cut them the night before in his hurry to get away from the flash flood.

After Preston relieved himself and brushed his teeth, Damien gave him his tablet while he worked, and the meditation time helped, but as the sun rose higher in the sky—and the heat became more and more oppressive—Preston got more and more impatient. He managed to wait until Damien was ready to go before he begged him to check the satellite phone for a message from Glen.

"Nothing from Glen," Damien said, looking. "But Buddy left a text. He said he found someone with a crop duster near where he's camping out. If we can find a strip to land the plane, he can fly it here."

"I haven't seen anything like that," Preston said. Scrub on the side of the mountain, trees on the ridge, and the road that was a five-foot swath of dust at its most generous. "There was nothing on the satellite either."

Damien frowned. "I wonder…." He bit his lip and texted for a moment, smiling when he got the answer back. "Good." He texted again, then turned the phone off to save power. "I asked him to be ready to fly one of us to Las Varas. Buddy can fly a plane fine, but he doesn't know squat about choppers. If we need to relay to get to the helicopter, Buddy'll be ready."

He put the phone back in his duffel and double-checked the packing before giving all the horses an alfalfa cube for energy.

"You ready for help on the horse?" he asked, and Preston tried not to groan.

"This show's gonna be better than your show," he said glumly.

Damien had no idea how graceful he was, even when he was struggling with his injury. Preston felt like a tree—and it was worse now with his shoulder sending shooting pains to his neck every time the bones rubbed together. His wrist was one big swollen ache too.

"Here. Let's walk the horses for a bit. See those rocks up the trail? I've got an idea."

The boulders were scattered on the downslope of the mountain like God's marbles, and Preston was pretty sure he knew what the idea was. Sure enough, Damien led Chewie to a medium-sized boulder, one Preston had no trouble climbing, even without his hands. Once there, Damien held the horse still while Preston lay down on his stomach across the saddle and then swung his leg around so he was facing forward.

"I'm going to hold on to his reins too," Damien said. "If I had a saddle, I'd tie them to the pommel, but I don't, so it might be slow going for a little. Once we get to Hole in the Rock, maybe we can buy a new saddle, or find another way to get you back to where Buddy's waiting with the trailer."

Preston shook his head, feeling useless. It was the logical thing to do. He was going to slow them down on horseback, and they didn't even know how Glen was doing. But he didn't want to leave Damien. He knew it was superstition—he *knew* Damien wouldn't just ghost him—but he finally had him. They'd finally been together, and Damien seemed to want to stay. More than that, Damien seemed *happy* to stay. Joking and bullshitting and teasing. The Damien that Preston had first been attracted to like a lodestone was there with him. Preston didn't want to jinx that in any way, and dammit, riding a horse with broken bones *hurt*.

A thing Damien seemed to know instinctively, as he set their pace a little faster than a walk, a little slower than a canter. Preston held on with his knees and thighs, bracing with his core until he thought his stomach muscles were going to pop out of his back. They both knew he was toast if Chewie decided to rear up or give them any trouble whatsoever, but Damien had such a handle on SnakeEyes that his horse didn't even look back to nip.

Preston could only be grateful.

They rode steadily, and broke to water the horses and have a snack about two hours in. Preston stayed on Chewie's back, because no matter how bad his ass was aching, the fire in his collarbone and wrist was even worse. The sun was just starting to get high when the terrain around them changed just a little, leveling out so the road widened. What appeared to be businesses on either side—many of them modest buildings made of wood and brick—were no longer standing, including a larger building at the end of the road that might have been a brick church, once functional and friendly.

Today, all of them were collapsed, as well as most of the buildings on the street.

The church had been large enough to hold the entire town, and what looked to be half the population was outside, rooting among the rubble and calling out names.

"The whole town," Damien murmured. "Holy wow."

Preacher gave an excited bark at the new people, and then he whined, pawing the ground like he wanted to work.

"They're trying to find survivors," Preston said softly. Or bodies. "Damien, tell them to let Preacher help!"

Damien sped the horses up, then came to a stop in front of the large group of people in front of the church, most of whom had paused in their rescue efforts to turn toward him. He spoke rapidly to the crowd, and a middle-aged woman wearing tattered jeans and a T-shirt stepped forward, wiping sweat from a face made haggard with lack of sleep and worry. Damien talked to her intently, and she nodded a couple of times, then spoke to the crowd. All of them looked at the dog and then at Preston, with his arm in a sling. Preston raised his bandaged wrist, and a few of the larger men stepped forward, arms raised, and Preston looked to Damien, who was sliding off his horse stiffly, the discomfort of the ride without the saddle marking every move.

"What do they want?" Preston asked, feeling helpless. He wasn't great with words anyway, but he didn't even speak this language.

"Trust them," Damien said. "They'll catch you. Just lean sideways and they'll help you off the horse."

Preston swallowed and wondered if this was how Damien felt when Preston asked him to trust that they could be together. He was putting himself in the hands of people who might not be able to catch him.

Preston could catch Damien—he had to have a little faith.

He shifted his weight to the left, and the arms lifted into the air caught him, being very careful of his injured shoulder as they lowered him to the ground.

Oh, the blessed, blessed ground.

He actually stomped his feet a couple of times, trying to stop that subtle feeling of movement from making him wobble. Horses. Chewie had been great for the last bit, but Preston was a long way from being excited about getting back in the saddle.

Damien's steadying hand on his good shoulder helped him get his bearings. "We'll start around the church," he said softly. "Because it collapsed during the first earthquake. But your brother and Cash were last seen near the general store yesterday morning. It's the only place with cell reception and…." He grimaced.

Preston didn't even have to ask what that face was. "The aftershock hit when he was texting us." He swallowed. "Glen's smart," he said.

"And Cash sounds like a survivor. Let's let Preacher do his job here first, and go check out the store."

A hard decision. Probably the right one, but not an easy one to make.

Preston took a deep breath and whistled sharply for his dog. "Can you get the treats out of Sunshine's packs?" he asked. Preacher showed up at his feet, and Preston held his bandaged hand like there was a reward between his fingers and gestured toward the church. "Preacher—mark!"

And that was it. Preacher took off, sniffing and whining. Within five minutes he'd stopped at a sloping rise that indicated a fallen wall. He barked three times and sat, pawing at the ground nearby, and Preston shouldered Damien happily on his good side before going to give his boy a reward.

Damien called out to the woman he'd spoken to, and she marshaled the townspeople. As a group, they gathered under what was left of the wall supports and lifted, creating a tiny triangle of space between the wall and the debris underneath it.

A child was the first one to crawl out, sobbing and battered, but alive.

Then a roar went up from the township, and Damien grabbed one of the beach towels and a bottle of water, then handed them to the tearful man—possibly a relative—who had helped the child emerge.

Preacher barked again, and another child came out, followed by a mother, and two teenagers behind her.

Damien pulled supplies for each of the victims, and Preacher paced and whined in an anxious circle.

"Good boy. Leave it. You can leave it now. We're good." Preston fondled Preacher's ears and gave him another small treat, and then whistled again and gave the command, "Preacher, mark!"

Two more times Preacher found a place in the rubble that housed an air pocket, and six more people were helped out. Preacher loved finding live targets—the children, in particular, wanted to pet him, lavish him with love, and Preacher licked their faces, much as he'd licked Preston's the night before.

Comfort. It was the lesson all dogs knew in their bones.

And it was needed—because the dogs trained in search and rescue got depressed when their targets didn't move. The dogs used after the 9/11 disaster had needed people new to them to pretend to be lost so they could find someone and know that people could be okay.

Preston tried not to hold his breath and hope that Glen would be a happy find and not a sad one.

In the meantime, Preacher circled the church once more as Damien and the woman in charge conversed about who was left.

"One more," Damien said. "Preston, there's one more person in there—"

And then Preacher went to ground.

He dropped, resting his chin on his paws, and whined. *Oh no.*

He was better at finding live targets, but Preacher was a smart dog. He knew the signal for targets that weren't moving.

"Damien?" Preston hated that signal.

Damien took a look at Preacher's attitude and nodded soberly. "I'll tell her," he said. "They're missing an elderly man. I don't think they're surprised."

And with that, Damien spoke in low tones to the town's leader, his face a study in compassion. The woman's face crumpled, and Preston's stomach churned. Oh, poor woman. This man was someone she'd loved. Damien squeezed her shoulder, and she launched herself at him, sobbing. He held her for a moment, because he was all that was kind, and called out to one of the men helping people from under the last spot Preacher had found.

The man trotted over—he must have been the woman's husband because he wrapped his arms around her shoulders and issued some sharp orders to the people around them. The remainder of the searchers moved to where Preacher whined, his depression at finding a nonviable target palpable.

Damien and Preston locked eyes, and Damien turned toward the woman's husband, speaking quickly. The man nodded and jerked his chin toward a solid building about two hundred yards away. Damien moved to where Sunshine was standing patiently as rescue workers pulled out water and beach towels from her travois, and he gathered up a bag full of water, saltines, and beach towels for himself. Then he looked at Preston and nodded.

Preston whistled sharply, twice, and gestured with his bandaged wrist toward the building.

"Preacher, mark!"

Preacher leapt up from his vigil by the church and went loping off into the distance. Preston pulled in a painful breath.

"I hope he only does that once," he said softly.

"God, me too," Damien muttered. "Glen, you asshole, you'd better be okay."

Preacher started barking excitedly, bounding around the demolished store with his tail wagging.

Damien and Preston looked at each other with painful hope and began a slow jog toward the ruins.

Love on the Run

"DAMIEN, you asshole, I know that's you out there! Preston, come get your fucking dog and let me out of here!"

Glen's voice, echoing out from under a downed wall, was one of the sweetest things Damien had ever heard. Well, besides Preston's voice after Damien had come down from the mountaintop, that is.

"Glen!" Damien called out as he neared the fallen structure. "The fuck you doing there, man!"

"Trying not to bleed out. What sort of asshole question is that?" Glen sounded weak and irritated, and while the weak was worrisome, the irritated was a blessing.

It meant he was okay for the moment, and Damien could work with that.

"Preston, your brother's an asshole," he said as Preston drew near.

"I knew that. Is he okay?" Preston sounded winded, and Damien figured between the altitude and the pain, he probably had the right to be.

"He's hurt!" came a man's voice, younger than Glen's and shaky. "His shoulder's squashed and bleeding, and he's hot."

"Dammit, Cash, I'm fine," Glen said, but he didn't sound convincing.

"You're not, and it's my fault."

Damien raised his eyebrows and looked at Preston, who shook his head. Neither of them was going there. Whatever was happening between Glen Echo and Cash Harper was obviously not their jam.

"I'm gonna lay this one at the feet of God," Damien called, because judging from the layers of debris, Damien had enough work to do. It appeared a wall had fallen wholesale—no breaking or convenient crumbling. He was going to have to lift up a corner and see if Cash and Glen could be pulled out from under the entire thing. But if the wall had fallen *on* Glen, things could be tricky. "Now, guys, someone needs to tell me where to lift so I don't squash you!"

"I'm pinned under a counter at the southeast corner of the building," Glen called. "Cash is mostly under a metal shelf. It's protecting him from most of the pressure, but I've got half the goddamned building on my shoulder."

"What happens when we lift from the southeast?" Damien asked, searching the rubble for leverage to try just that.

"It all shifts to his back!" Cash called out.

"So that's a bad idea." Damien moved to the other side of the wall, where Preacher was digging frantically. "How about here?" He bent his knees and tried a corner of the wall, ignoring the pain in his leg and lifting with his shoulders, back, and core.

"Augh!" Glen's scream, ripped from a shredded throat, made him stop in a hurry.

"Okay, then. Fuck." He closed his eyes, envisioning the problem. The wall was resting on the counter that was resting on Glen—he needed it to rest on something higher. *Think, Damien, think!* "Fulcrum," he said after a moment. "We need a fulcrum next to Glen that will take some of the pressure when I lift from here. Cash, you got anything?"

"The shelf I'm under would wor—"

"Don't you fuckin' dare!" Glen panted. "All the fuckin' trouble I went to, keeping you safe?"

"Not worth it," Cash sobbed, and Damien growled.

"Shut up, Cash. Glen says you're worth it, you're worth it. Now hold up. I see some cinder blocks."

Oh God—heavy. He dragged the first one to the corner of the wall and shoved it in, then got down on his stomach and peered into the darkness until he spotted a pile of dusty, blood-stained khaki shirt.

"There you are, asshole," he said into the sweltering cave of debris. "Thought you could get out of work next week?"

"What are you doing down here, gimpy?" Glen asked, turning his head so Damien could look into his hooded blue eyes. So much like Preston's, but with a big dose of snarky bastard where Preston had directness, and a little dash of snake-shit mean. "Why isn't my gigantic brother helping you out?"

"He fell off another goddamned horse," Damien told him, shoving at the cinder block until Glen grunted as it pushed against him. "Broke his wrist and his collarbone."

Glen's shoulders shook under the weight of the wall. "Fuckin' figures. Tell him to stay off the damned things."

"No, no—he's got plans. He's gonna get them for the ranch. We're gonna go riding together." Damien kept talking, because if he and Glen were talking, Glen wasn't hurting.

"Invite me to the wedding. I'll try to be busy that day."

"You'll be the best man and love it. Now shut up. I'm going to get another block."

He wiggled out of the crawlspace and pushed himself up, ignoring the embarrassment of the bad leg and hunting for another block. Preston had sighted one for him, and kicked at it futilely.

"I'm goddamned useless," he burst out.

"Keep finding more of these," Damien told him, hauling at this one. "You're worth your weight in gold."

"Preston sounds pissed off," Glen said as Damien pushed the cinder block under. "Didn't get his morning ritual?"

"Morning ritual doesn't make him feel less helpless," Damien muttered. "God, this thing got heavier. How you doing?" He reached into his pocket and pulled out the bottle of water he'd shoved there before getting the block from Preston. "Here—can you grab this?"

Glen grunted. "Shove it up over my head. Cash is stuck there. He can grab it."

Damien did as ordered, and a dusty hand appeared to take the bottle. After a moment filled with Damien shoving the cinder block forward to match the other one, he heard Cash's voice. "Turn your head, Flyboy. I'll get you some water."

Damien bent double, resting his back against the wall, and pushed up against the ground, his back taking some of the weight off Glen's, and Glen did as requested. "Thanks," he muttered. "How's the plan coming, Damie? This shit's getting old."

Damien fell forward into the dust, grunting, and Glen grunted as the full weight came back. "One more block and I think we can lift this wall without making you into lunchmeat—I know you're sad about that."

"My driving ambition," Glen said, voice as dry as the dust that choked him. "God, when'd you get your bitch back? I missed him."

"Six hours in a cockpit with your damned brother. Blame him!" Damien had missed this, this sparring, this play. God, he really had to get Glen out of there so they could bitch at each other as old men.

Glen's chuckle was weak but evil. "Finally. Jesus, you two. Fucking finally."

One more cinder block and a couple of two-by-fours and Damien was ready. Or he thought he was.

As he made ready, Preacher dancing at his heels, to use one of the two-by-fours as a lever to shove the wall up off Glen's shoulder and legs, he was conscious of movement by his side.

The townspeople who had worked to get their own families out from under the collapsed church were there, two taking the board from Damien, several others squatting to lift the wall itself. Damien dropped back, exhausted, and looked over at Preston.

"You?" he asked.

Preston shrugged. "I just waved a lot and gestured. They were smart enough to figure out we needed help."

Yeah, but Preston had reached out to other people—people not his family. It was a big deal.

"Thanks," Damien said, winking tiredly. Then he took one end of the two-by-four and called out, "Ready? Uno! Dos! Tres!"

And as a single unit, they lifted the wall.

People stronger than he was were doing most of the lifting, so Damien scrambled down and pulled Glen out, grimacing as his friend gave an agonized yell when Damien extended his arms. As Glen's shoulders emerged into the sunlight, a smaller man scrambled out and took Glen's hips, both of them clearing the wall.

"Is that it?" Damien asked, panting. "Nobody else in there?"

"The owner got out right before the wall came down," Cash managed, falling to his backside with a thump. Damien peered at him, knowing him only by reputation as a pop singer. His shaggy sandy-brown hair and doe-brown eyes were dimmed by dust and some bloody scrapes, but even under the pain and fatigue, Damien could see he was a good-looking kid.

And the way he was gazing at Glen, with a combination of yearning and sadness, about broke Damien's heart.

Damien took a deep breath and realized they weren't out of the woods yet. "How we doing?" he asked Glen, and Glen, lying on his back and covered in dust, took a deep, shuddering breath.

"Been better, brother," he confessed quietly.

Damien took stock. Glen's shoulder looked pulpy and bruised through the tears of his shirt. Damien would have to wait for the town's doctor to come take a look, but he'd seen the wounds on his back, and they hadn't looked good. He'd left a lot of blood back under that demolished wall—Damien hadn't missed that. Under the grime, his face had a waxy, peaked look that didn't bode well.

Damien put his hand on Glen's forehead and shuddered. Not cold. Not cold at all. His hand came back damp, and he looked around the town.

"Preston," he said, trying to think. "Can you build a campfire and set up the water pots? We're going to need to sterilize a lot of water to clean people's wounds."

"Will do," Preston said. He moved and grimaced, the fact that he didn't even have one hand really hitting him hard. "Can you ask someone to help me?"

Damien nodded and called out the request to Dolores Perez, who was apparently the town's mayor. It had been her grandfather who had died in the church—but also her grandchildren and daughter who had been the first people to escape.

"Sí!" she called, and then turned to one of the older children of the village and nodded at him, pointing to Preston.

When she was done, Damien nodded her over and spoke to her in Spanish. He had the feeling she might know some English, but she was tired and frightened and he was a stranger. He stuck to the language that would help her feel safer.

"The water downstream was contaminated," he said briefly. "I wouldn't treat any wounds with it. We're building a fire to boil some, but we can't do it alone."

Her eyes widened, and she called out rapid-fire instructions across to the rest of the townspeople. Damien took a deep breath, feeling glad he'd stopped a potential health risk, but still not happy.

"There's no place to treat you," he said to Glen, looking around. "Like—no place to treat you. I gather the doctor's office was used for kindling last night, after the second quake. We brought supplies, but there's only so much you can drag up a mountain on the back of one horse."

Glen grunted. "Most of the buildings were standing when I texted you," he said ruefully, looking around. "That aftershock took us all by surprise."

"Yeah, well, I'd ask what in the fuck you were doing back here, but I don't want to start anything." He looked meaningfully at Cash, who looked away.

"I… I was looking for someone," he said gruffly. "My friend. She's up at Tranquila Paz."

Damien's eyebrows went up. "Tranquil Peace? Sounds like the name of a cemetery. Is that the McMansion we saw on the satellite pics?"

"It's supposed to be a retreat for stressed-out celebrities," Glen rasped. "But Cash escaped and called his manager."

"It's a *cult*," Cash spat, "and it's run by some asshole who calls himself Tranquilo, who's not even as Mexican as I am!"

Damien blinked. "Tranquilo? For fucking real? This sounds very Batman, and you just made my head explode. Is that why you ran back from Las Varas? To get your friend out? Why didn't you tell Glen so he'd help you?"

"He was too busy sucking my brains through my dick so I'd fall asleep and he could escape," Glen muttered. "Jesus fucking Christ. Kid could spot an idiot who thinks with his balls a mile away."

Damien *couldn't* blink now. "Oh dear God. It's like you met your kryptonite."

"I didn't know!" Cash said, sounding sad and desperate at the same time. "I didn't know you were a good guy!" His voice dropped. "And that's not why I did that."

"Sure it's not," Glen said bitterly. He closed his eyes and concentrated on breathing for a moment. "What's your assessment, Damie? I know you have a plan, I just need to hear it."

Second time Glen had called him "Damie" and not "asshole" or "moron" or "dumbstick," and Damien was officially worried.

"Okay. Me and Preston need to get you situated on the bedroll with some sort of treatment. We may boil you to death, but we have to wash out your wound and try to beat the infection. I've got some painkillers and ointment that I can give you, but the big guns—the oral antibiotics and steroids and injections—all of that was in my saddlebags, and that got taken out in the flash flood down the hill."

"Flash flood?" Glen's eyes shot open. "Shit, Cash—do you think Tranquilo took out the fucking dam?"

Cash groaned. "Goddammit. Yeah. Glen, he probably got them all out of there. The dam was his last defense. He was going to blow the dam and then use off-road vehicles to get everybody to the secondary site."

Damien closed his eyes and opened them, looking at Cash with pity. "That may work for the eastern slope of this mountain range, but here you have to do it on foot or on horseback. And none of us—I mean *none* of us—are in any shape to go after your friend right now."

Cash nodded, his eyes growing red-rimmed. "I caused enough trouble as it is," he said sadly. With a tentative motion, he brushed some of Glen's filthy hair from his eyes. "I'm so sorry."

Glen moved like he would have caught Cash's hand and then gasped, because his shoulder was in no condition to do any lifting. "It's fine," he said. "Don't cry, baby. We'll find her."

Damien had to fight the train wreck in his head—
Glen? Glen Echo? The cold-blooded sex-lizard who
would risk his neck for a blowjob but didn't risk his
heart for anybody? He'd just been led by his dick over
hill and over dale, and he was telling Cash Harper it
was going to be okay? If they weren't sitting in the
middle of a disaster zone, Damien would have checked
to see if the sky was falling.

As it was, he had other things to wrap his head
around.

"Okay, we get you situated, and what? These
people need more supplies, and they need help. The
only way to get them in is the chopper—"

"God, that's like a whole day away!" Glen muttered.

"No." Damien looked at the sky, stunned when he
realized it was only a little after noon. "No. Buddy's
got a crop duster lined up in the little crossroads where
he dropped us off with the horses." Damien frowned.
"Where's your horse, by the way? And the dirt bike you
came up on?"

Glen rolled his eyes at Cash. "I don't know if I'm
the one who needs to answer that."

Cash looked down and rubbed his neck. "I gave them
to Tranquilo's guards?" he said, smiling ingratiatingly.

Damien just stared at him. "I know there's a story
here," he said, "but I'm so surprised you've lived this
long. I mean, two days ago I would have put money
down on Glen killing you for that alone."

Cash shrugged. "I… I thought they ran the stable."

"What stable?"

"You… you know. The stable that all small towns
have? Like a garage for horses? And you know. A
garage for the motorbike too."

"Glen, you need to make him stop."

Glen gave a weak chuckle. "If you only knew."

"No, I'm serious. Your new boyfriend is going to make my eyeballs dry out, and I can't have that happen."

"No, you can't," Glen told him. "Because you've got to ride a horse down the hill, then fly the crop duster to Las Varas and fly the helicopter back, don't you?"

Damien looked around, as though he could find another way. "And all before dark," he said. "I can probably land between the buildings in the town, but it's going to be hard to spot once the shadows fall."

"I'll ask the mayor to maybe build you some signal fires," Glen croaked weakly. Damien met Cash's eyes, his own full of sober resolve.

"You speak Spanish, Cash?"

Cash nodded. "Yessir. My mom's an ex-pat who lives in Jalisco. It's how I knew about Tranquilo Paz."

"Well, Glen and Preston are going to need you. I don't know what your thing is about taking off when there's help right in your bed, and I know you want to find your friend, but we can help you find her—"

"Brielle," Cash supplied miserably. "We've been friends since we were kids. I... I dragged her into this. The life. She followed me into rehab, and then we were supposed to come here and chill out and get our heads straight, and...." He looked at Damien in mute appeal.

Damien closed his eyes. "Young and lost and vulnerable," he said. "How many people were at Dumbstick Piss's compound?"

"Tranquilo Paz—"

"I'm not calling it that," Damien said, voice sharp. "And you shouldn't either. Not tranquility. Not peace. How many?"

"Ten? Fifteen?" Cash estimated. "I... I was only there for a week before I took off. They kept telling us we could leave at any time, but they wouldn't let us use the phone, and there was always something else to do, and they wouldn't let us sleep or eat—"

"Brainwashing," Damien said. Because of course. Of *course* there was a cult of lunatics up here in the wilds of the Nayarit mountains. "Okay. We will help you. If you think Dumbstick Piss blew the dam, that happened last night. There is nothing we can do about it, and we're not going to catch up with them now. These people—Glen, Preston, the townspeople—they need you."

"I can barely wipe my own ass—" Cash protested, and Damien wondered if that was going around.

"Well, find a way to fix that quick. That helicopter can take four people, and there's a Cessna Buddy can fly to the base of the mountains that can carry up to nine. We *must* get people triaged, we *must* get their status assessed, and we *must* get Glen someplace he can take antibiotics and get better. These things are nonnegotiable."

He double-checked Cash's situation and saw that the kid was starting to fade out. It might have been shock, or it might have been reality. Either one. "You need to get stitched up. Don't think I don't see the cuts on your head and forearm. You're bleeding pretty heavily. So these are our needs: we need to see who needs medical attention, and we need to see if there's anyone besides Glen who needs a hospital. There is a lot to do, and I'm going to be riding a bitchy-assed horse down the fucking mountain to get it started. Preston can barely move—he needs a cast and some serious drugs and probably some antibiotics too. So you're it, kid. You're what these people got. I have to leave the two people I love most in the world in your hands, and you had better not fuck this up."

"Aw," Glen rasped into Cash's glassy-eyed silence. "You love me."

"I love that bitchy-assed horse too," Damien retorted. "Don't read anything romantic into it."

"What about my brother?" Glen asked, and if the sarcasm didn't seem to be the only thing keeping him conscious, Damien would have told him to shut it. "Should I read something romantic into *that*?"

Two water bottles and a beach towel appeared at Damien's side. Damien looked up to see Preston standing next to them, taking in their conversation with wide eyes.

"You can read anything you want into it," Damien told him, dumping some of the water onto a clean corner of beach towel. "I'm not telling you shit."

"We slept together," Preston blurted. "It was great. He was the best I ever had."

Glen's tortured laughter echoed over the noise of the bustling townspeople and recovering victims around them. He closed his eyes against the brightness of the sun, which sat so directly overhead, there was no shading him. "Of course he was. You've been waiting for Damien your whole life."

"We're going to live together and be happy," Preston told him, jaw out stubbornly. "Beat that. I dare you."

Damien guffawed and started wiping down Glen's face.

"Here," Cash said quietly. "I'll take over."

"Good. I want to get him to the shade before we roll him over and strip off his shirt. I want a look at his shoulder before I go down the hill, and we need the doctor to help."

"Make sure he gets those cuts on his arm," Glen mumbled as Cash touched his face gently with the cloth. "Sweet touch, kid. Now watch my brother make cow eyes at Damie and report everything you see. It's my job to give him shit about it later."

"*You* are lucky you have people who'll come for you," Cash replied tartly. "You should try being nicer to them."

"I came for you," Glen said, his voice suddenly stripped bare and vulnerable, his eyes still closed. "And look what you did to me, kid."

"That's 'cause I'm stupid." Cash was on his knees, washing all of Glen's scrapes, from the front of his shoulder to the big gash on his head. "A smart man would have known a good one when he grabbed him by the scruff of the neck."

Damien's heart ached for them. He suspected it was no easy road between the two men—but that was not his romance.

His romance was glaring at him with recrimination and hurt, and it was Damien's job to fix it.

"I heard," Preston said baldly as Damien took him aside and walked a few paces, until they were alone under a tree. "You're leaving us."

"I'm not leaving you!" Damien protested. "I'm going to get help!"

"It took us a whole day to get here," Preston argued. "How are you going to get down the hill and then fly back in time to help Glen! You're going to leave him here, and he's going to… to…." Not even Preston could say it.

"Glen's going to live," Damien said, because there was no alternative. "He's in much better shape than I was when I came down my own mountain. And we took a day to get here so we wouldn't destroy the horses. Chewie and Sunshine are trail horses—they don't have speed, just endurance. SnakeEyes was bred for hard-core riding.

Buddy told me she's done a hundred miles in a day before and woke up to do it again. She'll get me down the hill, and I'll be back by dark with the chopper. You need to keep your brother bitchy and brave, you hear me? You need to keep Cash from running, because sure as shit, once Glen's situated that kid's gonna take off. He feels like hell, and he doesn't have a lot of patience with himself right now. So they need us both, you got it? But we've got one saddle, and baby, I'm the one who can ride. You and Preacher were the heroes here today—now it's my turn."

Preston closed his eyes and grabbed Damien's arm with the hand with the bandaged wrist. "I don't like watching you go," he said nakedly, and Damien leaned forward to touch their foreheads together.

"I don't like going," he said. "I wouldn't do it if we had any other choice."

Preston nodded, and Damien ignored the townspeople and the chaos and kissed him—ravished him—slow, tenderly, like they had all the time in the world in the shade with the smell of dusty pine around them. He pulled back and made sure Preston was looking him in the eye.

"I'll be back," he vowed.

"But will you come back to *me*," Preston asked, and Damien couldn't dodge or pretend, not now.

"There will be other nights," he promised rashly. "I'm not sure how we'll work it out, but there will be other nights."

Preston kissed him softly on the forehead. "There'd better be," he said, and then it was time to get to work.

IT took them an hour to get Glen situated and triaged, while the townspeople worked frantically to pull water from the stream and boil it. Damien's kit revealed there were still pesticides—it wasn't safe for drinking—but once boiled it could be used to tend to the wounded and wash the sick.

At Damien's direction, they moved the people toward the side of the town nearest a copse of trees, so those injured could have shade and some comfort, and he got a detail on clearing out the center of the town—and setting emergency lights as dark fell—so he could land the chopper.

He spoke to the town's doctor, and they both agreed that Glen needed the most help, but there were three or four others who would also need transport—six total, including Preston, who Damien wasn't going to leave without.

Two trips, then, in Glen's little four-seater. Damien could do that—the light pollution was so low, he would just need a triangle of flashlights to show him where his target was. Two years ago, he wouldn't have thought twice about it, nor about doing it twice, and today? Glen and Preston both needed him like they never had before. It wasn't only that he didn't have a choice. He'd been telling himself that for a year. He didn't have a choice—he *had* to fly, because that was the only way he could make his living. This was different. It wasn't that he didn't have a choice, it was that he had a *need*. He absolutely, without question, *needed* Preston and Glen to be okay.

He needed to be the one to make them that way.

With that resolution, Damien rounded up the horses and rubbed them down, making sure everybody had some alfalfa and water. He patted Sunshine, who only wanted love, and asked her if it felt better now that she wasn't hauling the travois, and told Chewie

how good he'd been to get Preston up the hill. He
pulled out his knife and cut an apple into three pieces,
because the horses had done their share to get help to
the mountain village, and then he turned his attention
to SnakeEyes.

"Okay, so, Miss Eyes," he said soothingly, feeding
her one more slice of apple to see if he could get her
to be sweet. "You and me have a job to do. And I get
it. You've done the flood thing and the going slow
thing and the bareback thing—and don't think I don't
remember how many times you tried to throw me
either. But this is different. We've got people counting
on us. No more of your tricks, you understand?"

SnakeEyes tried to take a bite out of his hand,
and he shoved her head away from him. "No. No,
you nasty wench. I'm going to grant you your dearest
wish, darlin'. You and me, we're going to fly down that
mountain, you understand? You've had some rubbing
and some water and some love, and now it's time to
pour on the heat. You think you can do that for me?"

She snorted and tried to knock him down with her
shoulders. He pushed her away again.

"You mark my words, old woman. You are going
to love me by the time we get down that hill."

He looked over to where Preston sat under a tree,
awkwardly changing the poultice on Glen's shoulder
with the fingertips of one hand while Cash watched,
and laughed softly to himself. A little more than forty-
eight hours ago Preston had told him, in no uncertain
terms, that Damien *would* be his by the time they were
done. It seemed fortuitous, somehow. Damien *was*
his—in all the ways that counted.

He had a need to make sure they ended up happy.

He and Glen could search and rescue all they wanted, but in the end, this was his most important job.

He secured Chewie and Sunshine where they could rest in the shade and get water, and led SnakeEyes to where his family sat, trying for comfort in an uncertain world.

"You dead yet?" he asked Glen as he approached. "'Cause after all the trouble we just had getting up this fucking mountain, that would be a damned shame."

"Not yet," Glen mumbled, lying on his side, good arm extended as a pillow while his crushed and bruised shoulder was relieved of some of the pressure. "I've asked, though—apparently they won't shoot a man like a dog, even if he asks."

Damien hunkered down by him, resting his hand briefly in Glen's filthy hair. "Well, good. Smart folks. You need to live and deal with your own misery. It's only right." He ruffled gently. "Hang in there, brother. I won't let you down."

Glen nodded. "Haven't yet. Try not to fuck up your other leg, though. That would be damned inconvenient."

"I am saying. Preston has some interesting thoughts on how the business should be run, by the way. I think you should listen."

"I'm only feeding Preacher filet mignon once. Maybe twice. Okay, for a week."

Preston laughed, because that was his kind of joke, and then said, "He'll be fine with hamburger, if you can hire another pilot. Just saying. Damien can come home."

"Our apartment not good enough for him?" Glen asked. "Because the toilet is *not* a science experiment—I keep trying to tell him that."

"You would need a control toilet to make that work," Preston said in absolute sincerity. "He can use the control toilet in *my house*. I want Damien in my house."

Glen grunted. "I did not authorize any co-opting of my best friend into your home. We shall have to negotiate."

"No," Preston said bullishly. "There is no negotiation. Your best friend is my man."

"He has responsibilities," Glen argued, his voice growing slurred. "He's the only one who knows how to make my hangover cure."

"Then *you* should stop getting drunk!" Preston crowed, and Damien looked over to Cash, who was watching them argue with wide eyes.

"You need to take care of them," he said under their bickering as Glen tried to explain that his alcohol intake was for the health and sanity of all around him. "I'll be back in time, but if he stops bitching, he stops breathing, you understand?"

Cash nodded soberly.

"And Preston won't complain, but make sure he gets painkillers in an hour. He can only argue with Glen for a little bit. His tablet and his sudoku are in his duffel bag—it'll keep him from fretting."

Cash nodded again.

"And they both get cranky if they don't eat," Damien finished, aware that his voice was getting a little crackly. "Take care of them."

"Yessir," Cash said, voice rusty. "I'll be here when you get back."

That was as good as this kid would get.

Damien straightened up painfully, his leg screaming at him that he'd had quite a day already. He was going to move to hunker down next to Preston, but

Preston did that stupidly graceful thing where he rocked forward on his toes and stood, no hands necessary.

"See you soon," Preston said, his voice hard like he was making this not a choice.

"Absolutely."

"Then you'll move in with me," he said.

Damien tried to hide his smile. "Glen is going to need a roommate for a few," he cautioned, because he'd needed Glen after he'd come down off *his* mountain.

"Fine. Until he's better."

"You'd talk me into it even if I said no," Damien told him, and Preston scowled.

"You just need reminding of what good sense is. Now kiss me so I can taste you before you go."

Preston's hot breath on his face, the taste of him, angry so he didn't have to be frightened, irritated so he didn't have to be worried.

Brief. So brief. Damien cupped his cheek.

"Don't worry, baby. I'll be back."

He grabbed SnakeEyes's halter before she decided to go back and join her mates, and swung up into the saddle before he could think about what he was about to do.

One last wave at his family and he turned around and hit that horse's sides with his heels, spurring her on to a ground-eating gallop.

He had a job to do.

Faith

"HE'S in pain," Preston said, sliding back down the tree and watching as Damien and the horse disappeared down the road. The horse's hooves sounded muffled on the dusty trail of the village.

"He's been in pain for a year and a half," Glen said, the fractious note in his voice fading. "Haven't seen him happy in that time. Until now. Good on you."

"You have to let him come live with me."

Glen chuckled weakly. "Preston, let's say I was all for that. Let's say I thought Damien coming to live with you was the best thing in the world. Let's say seeing you and my best friend together was like all of my happy family fantasies combined. What exactly would Damien think if I told him to just go live with you and leave me alone?"

"That you loved him and wanted him to be happy," Preston said doggedly. Preacher licked his hand, stretched out under the tree with him after a job well done, and Preston reached down to rest his hand on Preacher's head. He really *did* deserve filet mignon, and Preston was glad Glen understood this.

"Mm… maybe. He also might think that I didn't love him and wanted to fob him off on my brother."

Preston frowned. "That's insane. You wouldn't do that."

"Yeah, but that's what he might think."

"Why? Why would he think that? That's completely illogical."

"People don't always know," Cash said from his spot beneath the tree. Preston had almost forgotten he was there. "Sometimes, people don't have someone to say it's okay, so they don't know. They don't know kindness is being offered until they turn it down."

"I forget," Preston said, although Glen knew this. "I forget that Damien might not know. I mean, how can't he know we want him? He's *Damien*."

Cash laughed hollowly. "Being who you are isn't always enough."

"It's enough for me," Glen said, and he sounded… sad. Wounded. Preston couldn't ever recall a time when Glen hadn't sounded full of himself and ready to take on the world. "Come here, kid. I'm… I would just like you nearby."

Cash made his way to Glen's side and took over laying hot bandages on his shoulder. "I'm sorry I dragged you into this," he said.

"I wish you'd been honest," Glen told him. "But I don't mind being along for the ride."

Cash was silent for a couple of beats while he finished the poultice. "That's actually a really nice thing to say, considering."

Glen's laugh was filthy, Preston thought. No wonder Damien liked to say Glen had guys falling to their knees with their mouths open—he could make something really sweet sound like sex when he was injured, exhausted, and burning with fever.

Preston didn't think that was a very good talent, himself, but his brother seemed to like it.

"Don't do that," Cash told him, surprising Preston. "Don't make it dirty. Don't make you being nice a dirty joke. That meant a lot to me!"

"Not that much," Glen said, sounding bleak. "You ran."

"That's on me," Cash told him firmly. "I... your friend Damien isn't the only one who doesn't know. Not really."

Preston had been fading them out, because their conversation really had nothing to do with him—but he perked up when Damien was mentioned.

"You think I didn't figure that out?" Glen snapped. "Jesus. I've been called a lot of things—"

"Manwhore," Cash muttered. "Jackass—"

"Don't stop there, sweetheart. You're just getting started."

"Well, the manwhore thing is something you can change," Cash told him.

"Right back atcha! But I was going to say, nobody's ever called me stupid. Until right bloody now!"

"*I never thought you were stupid*!"

"Just gullible, right, kid?"

And Preston was out. This was their conversation, and he didn't have anything to add. Worse, it sounded like they were sniping at each other as sort of a ritual, a comfort exchange. It was like he'd said to Damien. All those fuckin' words that didn't mean anything. When Damien talked to Preston, he said real things. He said, "Here's your tablet," and "Dinner in an hour," and "Don't worry, baby."

That last one meant the most.

He'd promised. He'd promised Preston he'd come back. Preston couldn't even wrap his arms around his knees because his shoulder hurt too much. He simply stared into space and thought about his little house with Ozzy and Belinda, and how nice it would be to move his room into the cottage behind it. He thought about Damien sitting on the couch that was there, his back to the corner, one leg down, and Preston sitting between his legs, both of them watching TV.

He thought about waking up to him every morning—or even a couple mornings a week, because Damien went overnight on jobs a lot.

He thought of days when all they did was go out on the ranch and work the dogs, Damien by his side.

They were simple things—he knew it. He didn't want to fly around the world. When he did fly, he had one or more of the dogs with him, and they were going to try to find someone. He wasn't a good traveler; he was a good stay-at-home-er.

But Damien there, next to him, turning some of his words and all of his honesty on Preston—that was the life he wanted to be leading. It was all he'd ever wanted.

Cash tapped him on the good shoulder and set his tablet in his hands. The battery Glen had given him for it was super special—it kept the damned thing charged for days, as long as he used it sparingly.

ﬀﬁ

"Thank you," Preston said, but he set the tablet down next to him.

"I'm sorry," Cash said softly. "I thought, you know, you looked bored."

Preston shrugged. "I was thinking. Planning. I use the tablet when I'm fretful. It settles my mind so I can make a plan."

"What are you planning?" Cash asked, and Preston felt so low, having watched Damien ride away from him, that he didn't mind telling him.

"I've got a ranch," he said, eyes shifting over the quiet of the mountain village. He could live here when it had buildings. It reminded him of the Sierras, with pine and oak and dust and not too many people—but it was much hotter than Napa, and that wind off the coast saved Preston's life sometimes. "I work my dogs every day. My friends live with me there in the main house, and there's a guest cottage behind it…."

He continued, outlining the life he loved and the man he loved, and how he would fit the two of them together. Cash sat, cheek on his knees, and listened, asking questions every now and then, and Preston talked like he rarely talked, even to Ozzy, who was his best friend.

When he wound down, Cash said, "That sounds like a really good life."

"It's the one I want."

"I've always liked traveling," Cash said apologetically.

"Then it's good you're with my brother," Preston told him, thinking this was the consolation prize of lives.

"Your brother's too good for me," Cash told him, and he seemed to be completely serious.

"You should drink water," Preston told him. "It's hot here, and we're all injured. We can get delirious if we don't stay hydrated."

Glen's weak chuckle told him he'd heard that, and that Preston had been inadvertently funny.

"It's true!" Cash insisted, sounding upset.

"Sure it's true," Preston soothed. "Damien and I wouldn't have come all the way up here to get him if we thought he was completely useless."

This time Glen's laugh was even stronger. "Preston, my brother, I should have drowned you at birth."

"You're lying," Preston said with confidence. "You blamed all the bad things on me when we were little. You would have gotten in so much trouble if Mom knew you let all the dogs out of their cages that one time." He turned to Cash. "We had fewer dogs then. Now not even a very fast boy could do it before we caught him."

Cash turned to him, entranced. "Tell me the story," he said, resting his cheek on his knees. "I like your stories, Preston."

Preston looked at Glen. "Glen should tell this one," he said, because he agreed with Damien—if Glen wasn't talking, he wasn't breathing.

So Glen started to tell the story of a very young Glen who thought all things should be free, and Preston watched the sky, waiting for dark to fall so it would grow cooler, waiting for the beat of chopper blades in the trees, waiting for the love of his life.

For some reason, after talking to Cash, he had some faith all three things would come.

SnakeEyes

DAMIEN was going to have nightmares about that ride for the rest of his fuckin' life, his heart pounding as he clung to the back of a pissed-off horse, hurtling down the mountain, his leg cramping the whole damned time.

That horse really did not like him on her back.

She did like to go fast, though, so as long as Damien let her run and steered her away from obstacles, she was too busy keeping her footing sure to try to whip him off her back. But Damien couldn't relax for an instant. His legs screamed in pain, both of them, because the one that wasn't injured was compensating. His spine hurt, his core, his head—all of him hurt from being jounced from head to toe for hours upon hours as he drove the horse to the limits of her endurance.

That alone would have been hard enough, but an hour into the ride, he came to the bend in the road where he and Preston had ended up the night before. The sound of rushing water hadn't abated, and as he slowed SnakeEyes, he could see that tree where they'd camped had about three inches of standing water around its base.

Something else must have given that morning—either that or there'd been a sudden rainstorm higher up in the mountains. Damien didn't know, but he did know one thing—this stretch of road needed to be passed.

He cantered SnakeEyes through the slow roil of water, dust floating on the top, and around the bend.

"Well, that's a disappointment," he muttered as he took in the small lake that had formed in the little valley where he and Preston had first camped. The standing water was wide enough to cross the road, forming a falls down the side of the mountain as it dropped off, and Damien sighted some of the debris swirling around on the top to see if he could gauge how rough the current was. He had to go across that current. Against it was easier, because you could at least keep your sense of direction. Going across would be rough—by the time you figured out the current had dragged you off course, you'd be tumbling down the mountain on the back of a horse, and that would be no fun at all.

At first it looked like it should be easy going—the top debris didn't seem to be moving that fast, but Damien and Glen had worked more than one disaster zone. He spotted a branch that seemed to be zipping along and squinted against the sun's glare off the water. Sure enough, it was attached to a larger submerged log that was caught in the undercurrent, and that thing was not playing. He watched as it reached the slight rise that marked the barrier on the side of the road before the cliff drop-off, and shuddered when it hit.

Then he shivered as it punched a hole through whatever soil had formed the rise and catapulted down the side of the drop-off, pulling a big rush of water behind it. As he watched, more of the road crumbled, hauling more water and more debris with it, and the good news was if this went on for any length of time, the short-term lake would be drained, but the bad news was any semblance of road would be gone with the water.

Maybe swimming across the current was the way to go. By the time SnakeEyes got to the trees, they might be on the other side of the wash, and that was where they wanted to be.

Damien stood poised for a moment, locked with indecision. Did he wait out the wash, knowing Preston was waiting and Glen might not have much time? Damien would have been dead in the first twenty-four hours of his crash if there hadn't been clean water, and that town was boiling water for a lot of people.

Or did he risk it? He used to be able to take those risks, fly that plane in lower than snake shit, land that helicopter where nobody else would go. Those risks were the ones that saved people's lives, and his belief in his ability to take them had kept him and Glen alive for a lot of years.

Now it might keep Glen alive, period.

Quickly he rooted through his saddlebags, making sure everything was locked down and waterproofed, in particular the satellite phone, because he would need to text Buddy as soon as he was through this wash. Then he grabbed the coil of rope and a carabiner, grateful rope work was something he was good at. Grabbing SnakeEyes's halter, because he didn't trust her not to just turn around and run the other way, he took them both to the tree line and secured one end of the rope around the trunk of a decent-sized pine tree and the other to the saddle. They were as far inland as they could manage, and the fifty yards of rope *looked* wide enough to cross the lake.

With a deep breath and a pulling up of his big-boy panties inside his damned uncomfortable jeans, Damien wrapped SnakeEyes's reins around his hand and led her into the flood.

A few steps and the water rose to his waist, that undercurrent pulling hard enough that he wondered if the tributary would be washed away forever, forming a new falls down the side of the mountain.

A few more steps and he was up to his armpits and didn't care. SnakeEyes whickered, threatening to panic, and he gave her reins a hard tug, reminding her that even if they were both swimming, he was still the boss. The water was cold—not the snow cold of the Sierras, thank God, but not bathwater, and he was struggling for breath as he tried to keep his feet on the ground.

Preston. Glen. He had to get across. Fucking had to get across. A branch tapped his weak leg and he went under. Fear washed over him, drowning him as sure as the water, taking his breath, his will. SnakeEyes yanked against his shoulder, and he floundered, knowing, just knowing, she'd drag him under her churning hooves, and there wasn't a damned thing he could do about it. His lungs fought for air, and he fought for balance, the current pushing him and the giant panicky animal he'd dragged into this mess closer to the cliff.

Helpless. So helpless. Exactly like he had been when his helicopter had been smashed against a mountain, and he couldn't do a damned thing to save himself.

Get up! He could swear it was Preston's voice in his head.

I can't!

You can too, you big baby. You know how to swim.

Or Glen's. With a frustrated push, he found the bottom, bracing himself with all his other muscles, his core, his back, his chest. He got hold of SnakeEyes and flexed his arm, keeping her in place as he pushed up on the one good leg, clearing the water and pulling air into his lungs. Standing on the tip of one toe and *willing* himself not to move with the current, he almost gasped. They were getting close to the edge there, and it was time to swim for the tree line.

"C'mon, bitch," he snarled at SnakeEyes. "Neither of us wants to go over."

They did it. One step at a time, they did it. They swam, they thrashed, they tiptoed, and they waded, but they stayed the hell away from the falls as they did it. They had just gotten to where SnakeEyes could walk consistently without her hooves being swept out from under her, when Damien hit resistance.

The horse neighed in confusion, and goddammit, the rope was too fucking short.

Damien was going to have to cut her loose from the rope and hope they kept making it to the other side.

He seized the rope, which was on her right side and that was too goddamned bad. He used it to steady himself against the flood as he mounted her back, and she was too excited about having all four hooves on the ground to buck him off. Once again he found himself fumbling for his Leatherman so he could saw through a perfectly good piece of tack.

When he had cut through the rope, he spurred the damned horse as hard as he could, seeing they were both sopping wet and he was wearing hiking boots. For once she didn't care. She took permission as a blessing and took off, her legs churning underneath her as she heaved herself through the water past her chest and then to her knees and then to her ankles, getting free of the hated flood. He had to slow her through the mud or she would have broken a leg, but the minute they hit dry ground, he let her go.

She was tired—they were both tired—but the sooner they put that madness behind them, the sooner they could get down this goddamned mountain.

They were both shivering in the aftermath, but the sun was baking down on them, and in the altitude, the sun had a head start. Damien was good in the mountains as a whole—but he was pretty sure the only reason Preston hadn't gotten altitude sickness was their slow ascent. There you go—a plus side. Needed that. *Keep moving, don't stop, don't freeze up, and don't think about the pain in your leg or the chafing all over your body in the wet clothes, because we've got three-quarters of the trip to go.*

When they'd both dried out and started sweating a little, he slowed her and gave her some water and half an apple for some energy, but didn't stop for long. Two more times, some water, a little bit of high-carb horse food for energy, and then they were back on the road.

He was exhausted—his leg cramping up like a sonuvabitch, his stomach cramping too, because the only food that *hadn't* gotten soaked and washed away was the apples, and he'd given those to the horse. His upper thighs were on fire where his fucking jeans had chafed from the wet fabric on the horse, and he really regretted giving up cargo shorts out of vanity.

He'd just had that thought when he realized the terrain was leveling out, and recognized some of the landmarks from the first couple of miles of the ride.

Only then did he remember to try the sat phone to see if Buddy was answering, and right when he was contemplating slowing the horse to a walk again, he rounded the corner and found Buddy, sitting on a camp chair in front of his truck.

"You look like shit, boy."

Damien burst out laughing and tried not to fall off his horse. "What in the hell are you doing here?"

Buddy grimaced and came up to take the horse's halter. "Have you ridden her docile? Jesus. What happened?"

"You didn't answer my question." Damien took a deep breath and tried to focus. Time. They were running out of time. Glen's wounds were infected, and there wasn't enough water. Time.

"Well, I had Miguel track your satellite phone. When I saw you moving down the trail, I took a chance and showed up to meet you. Looks like I figured right— Damie, how bad is it?"

Damien swung off SnakeEyes's back and almost fell. "Fuck." His weak leg was absolutely done for the moment, and he could only be glad he didn't need it to fly. "It's rough," he said, trying to shake some feeling back into his leg that wasn't screaming pain. "There were a couple of deaths in the village and some injuries. Glen's the worst off—crushed shoulder and feverish. The water's no good. They're boiling it—we think someone blew up their dam and probably their water treatment facility, and I don't even want to know what's going on with their wells. Anyway—they need food and clean water, and we need to get the injured to a hospital. And that includes Glen and Preston."

"Here, son." Buddy shoved a shoulder under Damien's arm and started walking him to the front of the truck. "We've got food, water, and some painkillers for that leg. I'll tend to the horse and get her trailered—she looks like you plumb took the legs out from under her. You can tell me about the rest while we ride."

"Where we going?" Damien asked, the idea of sitting on a padded seat the closest thing to heaven he could think of at the moment. His inner thighs felt liquid, and not in the good sexy way either. It had been a long time since he'd spent that much time on the back of a horse, and if there was any justice, he'd be spending twenty-four hours facedown in a spa bed before he had to do another freaking thing.

"We're going to a miracle," Buddy told him, gathering the horse's reins and heading for the trailer. "Given what you just told me, I'm thinking one of you boys blew an angel."

Damien thought about it. "Probably Glen. That Cash kid's cute as hell and really sweet. Definitely not the three of us."

Buddy's laughter carried back to him, and Damien thought maybe he should eat before he said any more about sex lives and angels.

A HALF an hour later, they were driving back through the arable land at the foot of the mountains, and Damien was trying to get his bearings. "We're going northeast—is this the guy with the crop duster?"

"Yeah, but we've taken the crop duster and done one better."

"Buddy, we don't have a lot of time. I need to fly whatever it is to Las Varas, get the chopper, fly to the village—twice—and bring people down the hill. I mean, I was going to have you get a doctor to meet me back where the road ends so we can set up triage—"

"Son, you are not hearing me. I said this was better, and better does *not* mean you flying all over hell and damnation to get those people out. Better means better—you just have to have a little faith. We've been working on this thing since you texted me last night. You'll be very impressed."

When Damien first saw it, still dripping from a recent washing, its fatigue-green exterior absorbing the bright Nayarit light and not reflecting it, he thought it was a mirage.

"Where in the fuck—"

"It was in the guy's hangar, where he kept the crop duster," Buddy said, sounding insufferably proud of himself.

"Does it even work?"

"It flew out of the hangar to land by the side of the road," Buddy said. "But it's not all sparkly. See the bent prop on the tail? It lists to the right—a lot. You are going to have to fly the thing practically sideways to get it over the mountains, and the earthquakes have made the air currents a mite unpredictable, so tell me right now if you can do it."

Damien stared at the decommissioned Black Hawk helicopter in awe. He and Glen had one much like it back in Napa, but theirs had been taken apart and put back together to look like a limousine for the injured, with a complete medical bay and sound insulation and a cabin that separated the guests from the two guys in the cockpit. *Their* Black Hawk could handle six or seven people comfortably, and that included the two med-techs who worked Gecko Inc. as a side job.

This one was just as stripped down as a field-ready chopper should be. This piece of art could take eleven fully armed soldiers, complete with armor and grenade launchers and parachutes.

Or six or so earthquake victims plus a pilot and a doctor and Preston's favorite dog.

"Is it fueled up?" Damien asked, his heart beating fast with hope—and a little bit of fear. That bent prop was no joke, and landing this thing in the village and then taking off and flying toward the big hospital in Guadalajara was no picnic. "Can it make it to the village and then to the hospital? Or do I need to come back here and bus people to a field doctor?" He thought of Glen, barely holding it together. "I don't know if Glen's got another ride in him," he admitted, which was something he hadn't wanted to say in front of Preston, but he figured Glen knew.

"Nope—if you can ride this thing when she's bucking worse than SnakeEyes, we can get your people to the hospital in one goddamned go."

Damien spent the last ten minutes telling Buddy about his adventures and shoving more of Martha's beans and rice down his gullet with the help of homemade tortillas.

"You up for playing medic on this one?" he asked, because Buddy had some field medicine, and that was about all they had time for.

"I am," Buddy said. "But let's talk to our new friend Arturo—he's the one who's going to take SnakeEyes back to Las Varas for us. He may need a wee bit of recompense for using his chopper. And, well, for spending all night working on the engine so it didn't explode into a smoking pile of rust when we moved it out of the hangar."

People had to eat. Damien got it. "Tell him I'll buy it," he said. "Glen'll be fuckin' thrilled."

Buddy laughed. "You stay here and rest up some. I'm going to go drive a bargain."

Damien nodded and took him up on his offer. As he melted into the dusty front seat of Buddy's truck, he mentally prepped himself for getting in that relic from the '80s and pushing it all the way to medical service.

He did the math in his head, the vectors he'd have to fly in order to hit his target, practiced the compensation he'd have to do for hours in order to get his friend and his lover to medical care.

When Buddy returned, pleased as punch with his negotiating capabilities, Damien opened his eyes and looked at the chopper again, his ride through the flood with one pissed-off horse still fresh in his mind.

"You ready for me, you old bitch?" he asked, sizing up the vehicle with the eyes of someone who was licensed in almost every small aircraft known to man. "'Cause I don't care if the hand of God reaches down to give you a finger bang—you and me are going the distance or we're going to die trying."

The Black Hawk didn't do anything, of course. Just dried in the sun, looking vaguely menacing and only a little bit like it wasn't going to crash into the side of a mountain and kill them all.

But that was okay, Damien thought. This time, he was ready.

The Cavalry

PRESTON put his hand on his brother's forehead and shuddered. So hot. They were using cold water now, on his forehead, the back of his neck, trying to get his fever down as night closed in.

Glen wasn't bitching anymore, and Cash had taken to singing—mostly pop hits from Cash's own band, Preston assumed, but sung low and sweet and a cappella, they sounded more like, well, love ballads.

Glen had taken to humming in counterpoint, probably because he was too sick to know that was what he was doing.

Preston's wrist was swelling under his bandana. Cash had told him to keep it still—had been shocked to hear that it was broken, actually, and his collarbone too. He'd fussed over Preston until running that cold water on Glen's forehead was about the only thing Preston could do, which was just as well.

His body felt like shit. Glen was burning up with fever, and Damien had disappeared down the trail about half an hour before the people in the village had heard a loud explosion, followed by another whoosh of water down the hill.

"Secondary dam," Cash said. "Either it broke or Tranquilizer Piss blew it. I have no idea."

Preston managed to laugh a little. "Tranquilizer Piss—good one!"

"Well, Damien was right. Calling him that ridiculous name gave him this... this authority he didn't deserve. But he was paranoid; I saw that after a week. He could have blown the dam. I don't even know what it would do for him but make him feel safer."

Preston looked around the village, at the families tending to their injured and to the few dead who were being prepared for burial and being mourned. "These people don't care about him one way or the other."

Cash sighed. "No. They're just trying to survive." He sounded so dispirited, Preacher whined at him and begged for pets, which was pretty shameless, but Preston let him do that when someone was sad.

Cash fondled the big dog's ears and scratched his ruff. "Your dog is magic," he said, and he wasn't smiling or making fun.

"I know," Preston said, looking to the sky for the thousandth time. "We should put out landing lights, you think? The sky is darker now."

"You're staying put," Cash said. "Mind your brother. I'll go talk to Dolores. We'll find some flashlights and make sure we're not setting out a fire hazard. Don't worry. I'm not a complete fuckup."

"You're nice," Preston said, surprised that he'd be so angry at himself. "Don't worry about what you did to my brother. Glen's sort of an asshole to people. They don't notice he's nice too."

Cash gave one of the same smiles he'd given Preacher. "That could be the most awesome thing anyone's said to me," he said. Then he sobered. "Don't get up, Preston—you keep trying to forget you're hurt too."

"You hear that, Glen?" Preston said, smoothing more water down his brother's feverish forehead. "That guy thinks you're nice."

"He's so sweet," Glen mumbled, and he sounded sincere, which scared the shit out of Preston. "So sweet. Touch like heaven, that boy."

Oh shit. "Glen, you hear that?" Preston asked, his voice rising in urgency. "Think that's a helicopter?"

At first he only pretended to listen—he'd only said it to get Glen to snap out of it, to rally, to fight harder, because if Glen was being that sweet about *anybody*, he wasn't doing well.

To his surprise, he actually heard something.

Apparently, so did Glen.

"The actual fuck?" Glen asked, turning his head a little so he could try to watch the sky through the corner of his eyes. "Is that a goddamned Black Hawk? It sounds like *shit*."

Preston looked up at the sky right when someone turned on the Black Hawk's floodlights, and the search for landing lights became moot. The chopper was flying weird—almost sideways and not straight, even though there didn't appear to be any wind at all. There was a rattle coming from the damned thing that Preston didn't think a healthy machine would make, but there was no mistaking it.

It was big, it was equipped, and it was landing right there.

Apparently Damien had come to save the day.

The helicopter swung in a slow circle not once, but three times, before it finally decided on a place to land, well in front of the church, on the main street of what had once been the town.

The propellers began to wind down, and Damien and Buddy got out, a gurney between them. Keeping their heads low, they ran toward the campsite that was what was left of the town. Damien started barking orders for the able-bodied to get the supplies out of the chopper so they had room to put the injured, and Cash sprang into action to help organize folks who would do that. Damien spotted the people most likely in need of transport and started directing Buddy there.

Preston heard the words "Saving Glen for last, because he's the most injured, but let's get a move on."

Across the town, even as night closed in, Preston saw it when Damien searched him out by the light from a bird that really shouldn't have flown. He grinned, the expression exhausted and weary and cocky and arrogant and full of snark and positively brimming with self-confidence, and Preston showed all his teeth in response.

"Glen?" he said, knowing his brother couldn't look but wanting him to know anyway.

"Yeah?"

"Damien's back."

"He promised he would be," Glen said, because he obviously hadn't had any doubts.

"Yeah, but he's *really* back. Like really, really. Like 'so full of himself you want to smack him' back."

Glen gave a weak chuckle. "You okay with that?"

"I cannot fuckin' wait."

Glen chuckled again, and together they waited for their knight in slightly dented, slightly smoky armor, the guy who would ride a bitchy horse and a bitchier helicopter across a mountain range to their rescue.

Preston was going to make that man see sense if it killed him.

Damien spent some time making sure the right people got loaded onto the helicopter and getting the supplies sorted, because he was a hero and that's what heroes did. Preston didn't have to like it—he just had to know it was true.

Finally he came striding toward Preston and Glen, Cash and Buddy behind him with the stretcher. He was limping.

Preston rocked forward and stood up, his thigh and calf muscles screaming at him because he'd been doing that all day without sitting in a chair and his body was tired and thirsty. It didn't matter, because Damien stepped delicately around Glen and caught Preston's chin in cupped fingers, positioning Preston for a kiss.

Augh! So good. Warmth and weariness, confidence and care—all of it seeped into Preston's bones with that kiss, and he sighed a little, liking that Damien would take care of him sometimes too.

"Did you miss me?" Damien asked, his eyes alight with a wicked amusement.

Preston looked up and down his dusty, trail-beaten body. "Your clothes look like you swam in mud."

"I did. Most of the road is washed out, and it almost took me and the horse with it."

"Oh-oh…." Preston gave a little moan, surprised when his legs got soggy underneath him. "You almost *died*?"

Damien grabbed his hips and pulled him closer. "Don't get green on me now, Preston—we have to get into Buddy's cut-rate bird and fly to Guadalajara so your brother can get some treatment."

Preston nodded and rested his chin on Damien's shoulder, needing the support. "That's fine," he said, voice thin. "Because we'll be with you. But you don't get to do that alone."

"It's okay, baby," Damien whispered in his ear. "You were with me the whole time."

Preston nodded. "Because you know I love you, right?"

"Yeah. Because I know you love me."

That made it better. That was like Gran and Preacher's dam, Patsy, and all the dogs he'd loved but who had passed on, either to other people or to the dog cemetery by the tree copse on the ranch—they were all with Preston because he knew they loved him.

He was with Damien forever, because Damien knew.

"You love me too, right?" Preston whispered. He was pretty sure, but it had been a long couple of days.

Damien's arms circled his shoulders gently, careful of his hurts. "So much," he whispered. "You'll never know how much."

Preston probably did know—it was how much Preston loved Damien, but that was an incredible amount, and Damien could be forgiven for thinking Preston might miss some of that love. He had tunnel vision sometimes.

Behind them, Buddy and Cash arrived with the stretcher, and it was time to let Damien fly.

DAMIEN radioed a contact in Guadalajara for an ambulance that met them at the landing pad just outside the city. The hospital they were transported to was busy—efficient, but still recovering from the two earthquakes—and once Preston realized that Cash had brought his duffel, he had Cash put the orange service-dog vest on Preacher's shoulders, and the hospital staff promptly ignored him.

After that, Preston managed to stay with Glen until he was prepped for surgery the first time, although he was separated from Damien almost as soon as they landed. Damien, apparently, was the one who had to answer all the questions about where these people were from and whether more aid was needed, and specifically, where the hell the village was located.

Cash hung in there next to Preston while the doctors splinted Preston's wrist and set his shoulders in the collarbone brace, and then sat silent as his own hurts got treated. The whole time, he kept a quiet, comforting hand on Glen's head or arm or calf. Preacher chilled at their feet, practically invisible for nearly a hundred pounds of good dog. When they hustled Glen out of the triage room and into surgery, Cash threw himself against Preston's chest and cried, while Preston regarded him in silent horror.

But this was Glen's person—much like Glen had an obligation not to get Damien killed, Preston apparently had an obligation to let Glen's person touch him, even though he didn't really do that kind of thing.

It only lasted a couple of forevers before Cash fell asleep with a little hiccup and Preston poured him into his own seat to be left blessedly alone. He'd just pulled out his duffel with his sudoku when he heard Damien in the corridor, talking in rapid-fire Spanish to a rescue worker who was almost tearful.

In that moment, Damien popped his head in, took a look at Glen's empty bed and Cash's exhausted crumple, and met Preston's eyes.

"Baby, there's a collapsed building about a block away from here. You and Preacher are needed."

Preston swallowed. "What about you?"

"I'm flying supplies to more outlying villages—apparently they figured I could get some more work done after they banged that prop back into place."

Preston rocked to his feet and stood, tired in his bones. "Come back," he said simply, grabbing the little bag of Preacher's treats from his duffel.

"You too."

Preston nudged Cash carefully. "Hey," he said. "Me and Damien gotta go do hero stuff. Glen needs you here. You understand? You can't run. He needs to have someone in the hospital, okay?"

Cash nodded soberly, and together Damien and Preston walked to the hospital entrance.

"You'll get back to your sudoku eventually," Damien promised, weariness in his voice.

"I'd rather get home with you," Preston said. "Don't argue. Don't pretend it's not going to happen. Just agree with me."

"Sure. We'll go home together when this is over."

"We'll sleep in the cottage behind the house."

"We'll sleep in the cottage behind the house," Damien agreed.

"You'll come home three times a week," Preston argued.

"I can't promise that—"

"Three times a—"

"Not at first," Damien said as they broke into the dim sunlight of a fresh early morning. Preston breathed deeply and wished for the smell of long grasses, distant ocean, and dust from home. And if they were home, he wouldn't have to hear Damien make excuses while he avoided Preston's eyes.

"Why?" Preston asked, taking another deep breath of what promised to be another scorching day. He was too tired to work in this heat, but Preacher was needed.

"The three of us have a business, remember?" Damien said, and he sounded peevish and exhausted. Irritating man, doing all the hero things when all Preston wanted to do was sleep in his arms. "It's sort of what brought us here."

Preston looked up and to his surprise, Buddy's wife, Martha, stood there, in jeans with a kerchief over her straight black hair and a dust mask.

"Martha, you need to take Preston to translate," Damien told her, and she nodded. "Make sure he gets some quiet time and doesn't get his cast wet. I've got to run. Make sure he eats, and gets to talk to Glen, and—"

"And make sure you come home to me," Preston insisted.

Damien gave him a tired grin. "That's my job," he said. "I'm going to hug you now. Don't startle."

And Preston hugged him back, hard and tight in spite of his brace and cast. And a breath. And two. And three. Preacher whined and bumped his plastered hand, and Preston pulled away reluctantly, and that was all.

Ten hours later, Martha returned Preston to the hospital, so tired she had to lead him to Glen's room or he might have simply sat down and slept in a random spot in the corridor. Glen was sitting up in bed and drinking something sugary, his face set in an expression that Preston recognized only because he'd seen it on Damien's face for the last year and a half.

"Where's Cash?" Preston asked, collapsing into the chair at the foot of his bed. At his own feet, Preacher practically fell sideways.

"I'll get him some food and water," Martha said. "You too, Preston. You both worked so hard today."

They had. Not hard enough to save everybody, but Preston knew that wasn't possible. They hadn't made the earthquake—they could only help people stuck in the building.

Preston looked around again. "Cash?"

"Kissed me when I woke up," Glen said dispiritedly. "Said he was going to get some food. That was two hours ago."

"Did he get lost?" Preston asked, not understanding.

"On purpose, yes." Glen blew out a breath and set down whatever he was drinking so he could lean his head back against his pillow. "It was Cash Harper's way of saying goodbye."

"Well, it's a shitty way to do something," Preston muttered, appalled.

"I can't argue." Glen's hair had been washed before surgery, and his face cleaned. The scrapes there only emphasized what Damien had always called "roguish good looks"—but Preston could only see the sad.

"I'm sorry," he said, heart aching for his brother.

"Where's Damien?"

"Off being a hero some more."

"Lucky bastard."

"He needs to come home," Preston said, wanting home in his bones.

"We need to go there first," Glen said.

Preston nodded and yawned. Martha had laid out a cot for him by Glen's bed as they'd been talking, and with some gentle urging, she helped him lie down on it.

"When I wake up I'll get right on that," he slurred, and then he was out.

WHY, oh why, were things never that simple?

The next day, Buddy got Preston and Preacher on one of the first commercial flights home—apparently Damien and Glen had insisted.

Ozzy picked him up from SFO and drove the two hours to the ranch, where Preston fell asleep for nearly twenty hours before waking up in need of the bathroom, painkillers, and food, and having a hard time figuring out which order he needed all that in. By the time he got his bearings, over eggs and toast that Belinda had cooked for him, he finally managed to check his phone and saw that Damien had texted a couple of times to keep him abreast of things.

Moving all our planes back home. It's gonna take two days.

Flying back with the limo-copter in a few days to get Glen back to the apartment. He's giving the nurses hell. Still no word from Cash.

Preston texted him a picture of the kitchen, Preacher clean and asleep at his feet, sunlight streaming through the kitchen window. *Home.*

He managed an almost normal day that day before falling asleep early and waking up to another text.

Making a run to pay the rent. Getting in at dark thirty a.m.—sleep well.

Preston took a picture of himself naked in front of the mirror. *Home.*

Understood.

Really? Did Damien *really* understand? Preston didn't think so.

Over the next couple of weeks, as Damien ran around hell and damnation (as Buddy would say) trying to keep their business afloat, trying to get Glen situated, trying to take care of everybody but himself, Preston wondered if he really understood what Preston was trying to say.

He wasn't being subtle.

Got your brother here in the apartment, with a physical therapist down the street. When he can walk there and back, I'll feel better about leaving him here.

Preston took a picture of the dogs he was working, Preacher's direct descendent running with flopping jowls and a goofy expression on his doggy face. *Home.*

Mal and Tevyn needed a lift cross country—Mal fronted us the money for the new chopper no questions asked. Back in two days.

Belinda and Ozzy, working in the cottage, clearing out the old curtains, washing and painting the walls, laying new carpet. *Home.*

Checking Las Varas one more time for Cash so your brother doesn't fret so much. He's really hurting, Preston.

The cottage, looking new and sparkling, with a new bed in the bedroom and a new couch in the living room, leather, so the dogs couldn't cover it in hair. *Home.*

Training the new guys. One's an asshole, the other's a darling. Go figure.

Preston's wrist, plaster-free but wrapped in a removable Velcro brace, resting on top of Preacher's head. *Home.*

Four weeks after Preston had awakened in his old bed, he rolled out of his new one, put on his clothes, and went downstairs to fix himself breakfast. Ozzy came in, whistling as he always did, and plopped down at the kitchen table with a small pastry box carrying half a dozen donuts.

"You ready, brother?"

Preston nodded but didn't smile. "Yes."

"The men say it should be dry in two days—that's not long."

Preston nodded again, suddenly afraid. This was a really good idea—but what if it wasn't enough?

"He might not come," he said softly, hating to admit defeat. "All this… this motion. This noise. He might have forgotten."

"Naw," Ozzy said, pulling out his own donut and munching happily. "He's setting his world in order, Preston. You knocked it sideways, you know? He's making sure he can walk in a sideways world before he comes back to you."

Preston looked at his oldest and best friend, thinking that if Ozzy had kissed him back, Preston would have been really lucky and probably married to Ozzy by now, even if his face would never be as pretty as Damien's. Ozzy's heart was beautiful, and he didn't do all the noise and motion. They could have been happy.

"Will this help him walk sideways?" he asked fretfully.

"It will help him see that he always could," Ozzy replied. "Come, have a donut after your eggs. Then let's go do the thing."

Really, they'd done all their part the day before, cutting the grass, rototilling the area, and using the press to push it all flat. Now it was time for the professionals to come work. All Preston and Ozzy did today was assist the contractors and make sure the dogs didn't get out while the men were moving in the cement mixer and the lumber for the molds. Two days later, they came and took out the molds and installed lights at four corners of a perfectly sized concrete platform, situated far enough from the dog kennels to not drive the dogs apeshit whenever it was used.

There was also a neat sidewalk through the cut grass, straight to Preston's cottage. The men had been curious at that, thinking the concrete path would look better going to the main house, but Preston had been adamant. The big house was for Ozzy and Belinda and the baby they were still working on creating.

The little house and the path and the new creation in the southeast pasture were for him and Damien.

That night, at around nine o'clock, Damien sent him a text. *Glen says I need to get the fuck out of here—I'm driving him crazy.*

Preston sent him a picture of the new landing pad, complete with a big painted X in the middle and lights to illumine the way.

Home.

TWO hours later, as he settled himself sadly in bed, Preacher at his feet, he heard the violence of blades beating back the air.

And smiled.

Home

GLEN had not actually told Damien to get the fuck out of their apartment. No, with Glen there were usually more words than that.

"Oh my God, are you boxing leftovers?"

Damien paused as he was setting up the refrigerator. "Yes—yes, I'm boxing leftovers. I cook three nights a week, we eat leftovers three nights a week, and takeout of your choice on Sunday. This is how we've done this for years."

"Yeah, but Spencer's living here now—you boxing leftovers for him?"

Spencer Helmsley was their new pilot, and one of the reasons Damien hadn't moved out to the ranch yet. When Damien had been hurt, Glen had grabbed one of their Air Force buddies and put him to work. That guy had moved on to selling insurance in Chicago, because he liked the odds of staying alive better, so now, with Glen laid up, Damien had been on his own.

Damien had almost killed himself those first weeks trying to put their business to rights with half their birds down in Nayarit and Jalisco. By the time they'd surfaced from that and gotten Glen home, he'd been catching up on contracts. Glen was the one who'd started hitting up their old Air Force buddies to find a pilot who wanted a job.

Spencer had come highly recommended—sort of.

As a pilot, he was great—his marks were amazing, his job performance in the birds better than Glen's, if not Damien's, mostly because Glen liked to show off.

But there was always sort of a reserve as people were giving up his name, and until Glen and Damien met him, they were puzzled.

Turns out, Spencer Helmsley was the worst of Preston and Glen put together in one rangy, dark-haired, dark-eyed, closemouthed, handsome-as-sin asshole.

Also, he was gay, which Damien knew the first day when he'd asked if sleeping with his boss was a side benefit of getting hired there.

"No," Damien said shortly. "Not either one of us. I'm taken, and he's breaking his heart over someone, and if you so much as grab his ass, I'll break your fingers and throw you out of the nearest helicopter. Are we square?"

Spencer had grunted and crossed his arms over his enormously broad chest. "Touch-y."

"Exhausted. Can you or can you not fly?"

"I can fly."

"Can you or can you not get clients from A to B without setting us up for sexual harassment?"

"I can fly."

"Very funny," Damien had snapped. "Look—I'd like to see my boyfriend, and my business partner needs to stop fretting over this so he can recover. If you are not going to cooperate here, I know there are probably an awful lot of female pilots who would appreciate not getting their asses grabbed, so I will start looking in those pools."

Spencer had straightened. "My flight partner, Elsie—she needs a job. Would you really hire her?"

And Damien had cursed, because suddenly Spencer wasn't a douche. "Yes. Both of you. Do you both need the apartment or—"

"No, she's got a boyfriend in the city. But if you can get her a job that's in the air, I'll be an absolute Boy Scout, I swear to it. You'll never even know I get laid."

"Fine." Damien had sighed and closed his eyes, the pictures that Preston had been sending him kaleidoscoping behind them. "If she can start this weekend, I might get to go see my own boyfriend eventually, and brother, that would be something special."

"Good guy?" Spencer asked wistfully.

"He's not bad, considering he's related to Glen and Glen's an asshole. Let's get those contracts signed, and you can call your friend. I've got a good feeling about this."

So that had been it. Spencer had moved into the guest room, and Damien had taken over as den mother, getting Spencer used to how they did the schedule and keeping Glen from nagging them both into a coma. Between housetraining Spencer and wondering how an asshole like Spencer deserved sweet-as-pie Elsie as a partner, he ordered, begged, and cajoled the people around him to mesh so he could go see Preston.

"Damien," Glen said now, moving restlessly in order to not jostle his still healing shoulder, "what in the ever-loving hell are you still doing here?"

"Making sure you don't chuck yourself out of a bird?" Damien asked, only partly kidding. Glen's broken heart was as palpable as his broken shoulder and the crushed discs in his back. If Damien could have met Cash in a dark alley, he would have kicked the kid's ass, twice. Classy fucking move, leaving a man while he was in the hospital—for real.

"Jesus, Damie—you were a wreck for a year and a half—"

"And I believe we shared the same apartment then too!"

"Well, has it occurred to you that I want to know you're happy? You and my brother go have lots of sex and then invite me to the ranch so I can play with the dogs. It'll be great. Just… just go be his man first, my friend second."

Damien stared at him, waiting for the other shoe or the other snark or the other thing that Glen always had to say.

"That's it?" he said, feeling a little lost. "That's all you've got?"

"What's the worst that can happen?" Glen asked. "If you break up, you can always move back here with us bachelor losers. But you're never going to find out if you don't go."

Damien looked away. "I… what if…?"

"What if God picks up your helicopter and slams it against a mountain?" Glen asked brutally. "I don't know, Damien. You tell me."

"You suck."

"Not recently. Now go away." He turned his head. "Spencer, come here! We need to educate you on the fucking refrigerator. It needs to look like God's pantry before you think you're done with the dishes!"

"What's Damien doing?" Spencer asked, swinging in from the living room and looking disgruntled, which was the standard expression on his square-jawed face.

"Damien is going to text my brother and tell him he's coming home tomorrow."

Which is what Damien had thought too, until he checked his phone and saw the full-fledged helicopter pad Preston had laid out for him in the middle of the southeast pasture.

He showed the picture to Glen, his eyes wide, and Glen just laughed.

"Jesus, Damie, get the fuck out of here!"

It took him ten minutes to pack his bag, and Glen filed his flight plan while he was driving to the hangar.

He was going home.

HE landed the bird on the fresh concrete and turned off the lights before he grabbed his duffel and took the pathway to the newly refurbished cottage. He stood at the front door for a moment, conscious that Preston was waiting for him, and probably a little bit irritated at the delay.

Also conscious that Preston had sent more than one naked picture over the last month.

He swallowed, his throat suddenly drier than sarcasm, and knocked.

Preacher *whuff*ed low in his throat and the door flew open, like Preston had been on the other side, just waiting.

Damien stepped over the threshold, and Preston slammed the door behind him, wrapping Damien into a rib-cracking hug that said the brace around his bare shoulders was unnecessary. He was dressed for sleep in his briefs and his skin, warm and scented like country-boy fabric softener, and he enveloped Damien, made him safe, at the same time that hard, rangy body made him hungry.

Right when Damien was going to step back and say something snarky—"Maybe a kiss?" or "Surprise!"—Preston nuzzled Damien's cheek with his own, his breath hot in Damien's ear as he said, "I'm going to fuck you now. Don't startle."

In the time it took Damien's jaw to drop, Preston had spun him around, arms braced on the door, and was kissing his neck with aggressive openmouthed sweeps of his lips and tongue.

"I'd kiss you on your mouth first," he said, "but I figure you got talking to do, and this way I can ignore you."

Except Damien's body was melting, and his tongue was cleaving to the roof of his mouth, and he didn't think he had any words at all.

Broad, capable hands shoved his shirt up to his armpits and then pulled it over his head, and Preston resumed his kissing thing, his mouth on Damien's skin draining all the "wait" from Damien's body. Hard kisses, a hint of teeth, the feel of a rough tongue dragging down Damien's spine, and all he could do was turn his mouth into his bicep and moan.

"Don't you muffle that sound," Preston said brutally. "We're in the one place you can scream."

His hands made busy at Damien's belt buckle then, and the sound of his jeans hitting the floor and the cool air hitting his legs were almost a shock.

"Here?" he mumbled, but Preston was behind him, shucking his boxer-briefs down his legs and making disapproving sounds.

"What is this from?" he demanded, palms skirting the new pink skin on the backs of Damien's thighs.

"That ride down the hill, soaking wet," Damien muttered in mortification. "My jeans chafed sores on my legs—I was doing so much flying it took a while to heal."

"*And you're still wearing them!*" Preston snarled, and Damien kicked off his shoes and kicked the jeans away in response.

"Better?" This irritated sexual Preston overwhelmed him, dominated him, and without questioning himself, Damien would do anything to please him.

"Bend over," Preston snapped, and when Damien complied, Preston's big rough hands parted his cheeks, exposing him to the air, right before he dove in tongue first.

Damien moaned, not muffling the sound this time, his body blatantly possessed and invaded.

"You showered," Preston observed, but it didn't sound like it made him happy. "I've been waiting for a month and you *showered?*"

Damien was having trouble talking anyway—he wasn't going to point out the potential benefits while Preston was doing that thing... that thing with his tongue... and, oh my God, there went a big, blunt finger.

"Nungh!"

And another finger, this one spreading, and Damien's upper thighs started to shake.

"Augh! Preston! Oh my God—we need... oh damn... *gungh*...." Three fingers, and then Preston was fumbling with something, using the unoccupied hand.

The occupied hand was *very* occupied, fingers spreading, thrusting, massaging, and Damien had to work to support his weight against the door.

"I'm going to fall," he panted. Preston stood and wrapped a heavy arm around his chest, pulling him upright.

"No. I'll catch you."

Damien saw the lube bottle in his hand before he dropped it on top of the discarded duffel. Preston pulled his fingers out and Damien keened, mourning their loss. His body was shaking—thighs, bum leg, arms against the door. Preston's weight, his arm, his *will* were the only things holding him upright, and as Preston positioned his cock at Damien's stretched entrance, Damien had the thought that he was going to have to have faith, wasn't he? That Preston wouldn't let him fall.

Then Preston thrust hard inside and he didn't have any room for thoughts. There was only Preston's cock as it fucked him, hard, powerfully, slowly, and without mercy.

Damien's vision washed black, sweat prickling along his skin as he fought the urge to come.

"Do it," Preston murmured in his ear. "Come. I'll keep fucking you. I'll fuck you until you get hard again. I'll fuck you until you cry. Come. It won't stop me. I'm not done with you by a long shot."

A hard shudder racked him, grabbing Damien by the balls and taking over his entire body. That quickly, he shot, spattering against the door, and Preston remained true to his word. As Damien clung to the arm around his chest to stay upright, Preston fucked him again and again and again.

His cock swelled, spurred on by Preston's merciless thrusting, by the pressure on his gland, by the darkness and the pleasure of bottoming, and he reached down to stroke it.

Preston batted his hand away. "Still mine."

Preston took over the stroking, his thrusts and his hand coordinating to master Damien's body without effort. There was nothing to do but pant, beg, and scream.

Damien did all three, shaking, sweating, *needing*. He simply gave himself over as Preston battered, mauled, and loved him to the brink of another orgasm.

"I needed you!" Preston shouted as Damien's body hovered on the edge. "Stop being afraid!"

And the truth set him free. His body plunged off the cliff and his heart soared. "Not anymore," he gasped as orgasm swept him. It receded slowly, leaving him weak and naked and unable to lie with words. He slid against the door, Preston pumping inside him, glad for the come, not wanting their contact to end.

"You promise?" Preston whispered, his heavy body pinning Damien's and keeping him safe. "No more running? No more running around being everything except mine?"

"I promise," Damien mumbled against the door, his eyes burning. "I'll be yours. As long as you'll have me."

Preston grunted. "Stay right there. Keep your legs spread."

"Okay. Whatever." He had no idea what Preston was doing until Preston shoved his phone over Damien's shoulder.

There was Damien's backside, despoiled, Preston's come running down his thighs.

He straightened up against the door, more than shocked. "Preston, that's *porn*."

"It's *home*. And the next time you spend more than a week away from me, that's going up on my phone as a screen saver."

Damien gaped, turning around, his back against the door. "You can't—"

Preston took his mouth, hard and uncompromising, only pulling away when Damien was fluid and brainless and ready to concede to anything.

"I'll send you a copy," Preston said. "Every day you're gone more than a week."

"Okay. Okay." Preston wasn't kidding. Damien knew it. He didn't really need the threat, but he took it seriously. Preston didn't get embarrassed—not about sex. "No more running. I promise. Forever."

"Good. Now kiss me again. It's been way too long."

This time Damien kissed him, took over, reassured. This time Damien led, grabbing the lube and walking him backward to the couch that had shown up on his phone again and again, laying him down on it, throwing Preston's big, muscular legs over his shoulders and penetrating him slowly, being tender. Preston's crest hit hard and fast, because he was still young, but Damien was still recovering, so he got to take his time.

He got to see Preston's head tipped back, his eyes closed, his face relaxed in sex, in pleasure, giving himself over to the belief that Damien meant it.

He was there, in Preston's bed, in his home, in his life, to stay.

They finally made it to the actual bed, naked, sweating, spent, and Damien kissed Preston's big broad shoulders, tasting the salt of him as they both drowsed.

"This is a good home you made," Damien said softly.

"I made it for you."

"Us."

"Okay. Us. And the dogs."

"And the dogs."

Preston turned toward him and looked carefully at his expression. "What is that face?"

"It's love."

"Good. I like that face. Is that my face now too?"

"Yeah," Damien said, swallowing. "Yeah. That's my favorite face."

"Mine too. I love you."

"Love you too."

That's all they needed to say for quite some time.

Four months later

DAMIEN sat on the couch, e-book in hand, while Preston played on his tablet behind him. He'd come within a day of getting that shameless sex picture on his phone, and Preston had greeted him at the door in the customary way. They were wearing clothes now and recovering, but Damien was really not interested in moving.

And then his phone rang with "Danger Zone." Glen's ringtone.

"Fuck."

"Just did that," Preston murmured. "It was awesome. We can do it again after dinner."

Damien shook his head and pulled his phone from his pocket. Glen was cleared for short flights now, because apparently his guardian angel hadn't taken a complete break, and they still got together once a week for takeout. Generally he, Spencer, and sometimes Elsie seemed to be forming their own clique in the city, and while Damien was a little jealous of his best friend getting co-opted by other best friends, he was also happy for all of them. Glen seemed to be covering very well for his broken heart with sarcasm and beer, and Damien thought that showed a great deal more fortitude than he'd shown himself.

Their once-a-week dinner hadn't revealed so much as a glitch in their sarcasm—apparently Damien had kept his brother and gained a partner for life.

He'd doubt that his happiness would last, or even was real, but nights spent in Preston's bed didn't allow for any self-doubt. Anything of that sort had been burned away by their first fuck over the threshold. Preston's thorough possession of him, body and soul, allowed for no questions.

"Glen?" he asked, puzzled. Glen had shooed him out the door and into the chopper that night, telling him to get laid before Preston got cute with the phone.

"Cash just showed up at my door."

Damien stood abruptly. "I'm, uh, sorry?"

"He's found his friend. He needs our help. You guys need to pack your go-bags. Tell Preston we're going to need Skeet as well as Preacher this time."

Skeet was a dog Preston was training for the police force. His specialty was tracking down drugs.

"When—"

"Wheels up tomorrow at ten. Be here by nine thirty. Out."

Glen rang off, leaving Damien staring at his phone. "Ass. Hole."

"What's up?" Preston asked, standing and taking the phone away from him.

Damien laid out the situation, and Preston grunted, grabbed Damien's hand, and led him up the stairs.

"Where are we going?"

"To have sex again before we pack."

"The hell?"

"Wherever Cash is leading us, it's going to be an adventure. We need to have sex now so we don't miss it as much."

Damien laughed shortly. "We'll still miss it."

"Yes, but not as much."

Damien followed him, keeping his hand on Preston's back as they walked. "Cash has a lot of explaining to do."

"Yes, but that's him and my brother. That has nothing to do with you and me. You and me are getting married. He can come to the ceremony."

"We're what?"

"Don't argue. I'll plan. If you have to plan, it will just make you crazy. Me and Belinda have a list. We'll work through it when we get back."

"But Preston—"

Preston turned toward him with a wrinkle in his forehead. "Don't argue with me about this. It never ends well."

Damien had to concede to that one. "Well, we can hope whatever we're doing with Cash ends smoothly. Apparently I have a lot to do when we get back."

"Start now," Preston told him, mouth warm against his temple. "Get a jump on things."

Damien's chuckle was swallowed by their kiss, and any lingering doubts he might have had were soon to be burned away by Preston's hands, his body, his sex.

Damien's brain would spin or not spin, his words would come and go, but Preston's faithful, constant love would keep them together for as long as they both should live.

Now Available

 REAMSPUN DESIRES

Warm Heart

By Amy Lane
Search and Rescue: Book One

Survive the adventure. Live to love.

Following a family emergency, snowboarder Tevyn
Moore and financier Mallory Armstrong leave Donner Pass
in a blizzard… and barely survive the helicopter crash that
follows. Stranded with few supplies and no shelter, Tevyn and
Mallory—and their injured pilot—are forced to rely on each
other.

The mountain leaves no room for evasion, and Tevyn
and Mal must confront the feelings that have been brewing
between them for the past five years. Mallory has seen Tevyn
through injury and victory. Can Tevyn see that Mallory's love
is real?

Mallory's job is risk assessment. Tevyn's job is full-on
risk. But to stay alive, Mallory needs to take some gambles
and Tevyn needs to have faith in someone besides himself.
Can the bond they discover on the mountain see them to
rescue and beyond?

Coming Soon

REAMSPUN DESIRES

Home and Away by Ariel Tachna
Taking their shot at love.

University of Kentucky senior Kit Parkins has his life planned out. He'll graduate, get a good job, find a better apartment, meet the guy of his dreams, and settle down to a happy life near his brother and uncles, the only family he has left. But meeting Lincoln Joyner, UK's star basketball player, calls all his priorities into question.

Like Kit, Linc knows exactly where life is taking him: to the NBA and as far away from his hardscrabble childhood as possible. There's just one problem. He falls in love with Kit, who can't imagine life anywhere but in Lexington.

Can they find a way to keep their relationship going without giving up on their dreams?

Under the Covers by K.C. Wells
Can they find their HEA in Romancelandia?

Chris Tyler loves his job. He photographs some of the hottest guys on the planet, but none stir him like Corey Dayton. He'll never let Corey know—he values their friendship too much to spoil it.

Corey is looking forward to the Under The Covers Romance convention. It's a great opportunity to connect with readers who want to meet their favorite cover model, but more importantly, with agents who could advance his career. Too bad the only person he yearns to connect with is Chris.

What Chris wants is Corey in his life, but he's afraid that's sheer fantasy. What Corey desires is a Hollywood dream, but that will mean leaving Chris behind. What both crave is a real-life romance and their own happily ever after.

Made in the USA
Coppell, TX
14 February 2020

15825451R00129